Magic Ponies

Books 1–3

SUE BENTLEY

illustrated by Angela Swan

Grosset & Dunlap
An Imprint of Penguin Group (USA) LLC

GROSSET & DUNLAP
Published by the Penguin Group
Penguin Group (USA) LLC, 375 Hudson Street, New York, New York 10014, USA

USA | Canada | UK | Ireland | Australia | New Zealand | India | South Africa | China

penguin.com
A Penguin Random House Company

Text copyright © 2009 by Sue Bentley. Illustrations copyright © 2009 by Angela Swan. Cover illustrations copyright © 2009 by Andrew Farley. *A New Friend*, *A Special Wish*, and *A Twinkle of Hooves* first published in Great Britain in 2009 by Penguin Books Ltd, and in the United States in 2013 by Grosset & Dunlap. This bind-up edition first published in the United States in 2014 by Grosset & Dunlap, a division of Penguin Young Readers Group, 345 Hudson Street, New York, New York 10014. GROSSET & DUNLAP is a trademark of Penguin Group (USA) LLC. Printed in the USA.

The Library of Congress has cataloged the individual books under the following Control Numbers: 2012031918, 2012034127, 2013938726.

ISBN 978-0-448-48459-4   10 9 8 7 6 5 4 3 2 1

Magic Ponies

A New Friend

SUE BENTLEY

Prologue

"Wait for me!" Comet cried, launching himself into the night sky.

Moonlight gleamed on the pony's golden wings, cream coat, and flowing golden mane and tail. His deep-violet eyes flashed as happiness flowed through him. He loved playing chase with his twin sister.

"Hurry up, lazybones! You'll never catch me!" called Destiny. She swooped teasingly close and then shot upward to hide in a fluffy cloud.

Comet noticed the rainbow dazzle of a jewel on a chain around her neck. He gasped. Destiny was wearing the Stone of Power! The stone protected the Lightning Herd they belonged to and kept them all hidden from the dark horses who would like to steal their magic. It was forbidden to take it from Rainbow Mist Island where they lived.

"Destiny! Wait! Come back!" Comet ordered.

But his twin's laughter floated toward him on the still, cold air. Comet flexed his golden wings and zoomed upward in a spurt of speed. Soaring higher and higher, he burst through the cloud and emerged into star-studded blackness.

Destiny was just ahead of him. She turned, and her ears twitched with mischief as she folded her wings and prepared to dive.

Comet called to her. "No, don't! The Stone . . ."

Ching! There was a tiny sound in the silence as the chain around Destiny's neck snapped.

"Oh no!" A chill ran through Comet as the magic stone plunged into the lake below with barely a ripple.

Destiny's eyes widened in panic.

"What have I done?" she gasped.

"We must find the stone. Follow me!" Comet urged, flying down to the water and plunging in. Destiny followed him.

It was freezing cold and pitch black in the depths of the lake. The two ponies searched for a long time, but the stone was nowhere to be seen. Comet was ready to give up, when he saw a faint glimmer on the lake's bottom. With one final effort, he dived and managed to pick up the stone.

"I have it!" But Comet broke the surface to find himself alone. Where was Destiny?

The young pony quickly flew home to Rainbow Mist Island to find his mischievous twin and tell her that all was well.

As Comet landed on the island's lush grass, an older horse with a wise expression stepped out from behind some trees.

"Blaze!" Comet dipped his head in a bow before dropping the magic stone at the leader of the Lightning Herd's feet. It lay there glowing with shifting rainbow light.

"Well done, Comet," Blaze said in a deep voice. "Your sister acted rashly, but you have saved our herd from disaster."

Comet defended his twin. "Destiny meant no harm. I'm sure she means to say sorry right away. Where is she?"

"Destiny has run away," Blaze said gravely. "It seems she thought the stone was lost forever and was afraid that she would be in terrible trouble."

"But where could she have gone?" Comet asked, puzzled.

"We do not know. You must ask for the stone's help to find her."

As Comet looked down at the stone, it began to grow larger. Rays of dazzling rainbow light spread outward, and an image formed in the center of it. Comet saw Destiny's hooves touch down in an unfamiliar forest in a world far away.

The magic pony felt a pang as he thought of his twin sister: lost, alone, and in danger. He had to find her! There was a bright flash of dazzling violet light, and a whirlwind of rainbow mist swirled around Comet. Where the magnificent winged pony had been now stood a sturdy chestnut pony with a sandy mane and tail and glowing violet eyes.

"Go now, young friend," Blaze urged. "Use this disguise to find Destiny before she is discovered by the dark horses."

Comet's chestnut coat bloomed with violet sparks. He snorted softly as he felt his magical power building. The cloud of rainbow mist began to spin faster and faster and drew Comet in . . .

Chapter
ONE

"It's so gorgeous here!" Eleanor Gale exclaimed. "I can't wait to meet Aunt Pippa's new ponies!"

She looked at Oak Cottage, which stood on the edge of a forest. Roses rambled around the front door, and colorful flowers filled the front garden.

Eleanor's mom smiled. "Somehow I don't think you're going to mind spending your school vacation here while your dad and I are away."

Both Eleanor's parents were musicians in an orchestra. She'd had the chance of going on tour with them, but had instead chosen to accept the invitation to stay with her aunt.

"Spending all day riding or hanging about in boring hotel rooms? It's no contest!" Eleanor said.

Her dad smiled indulgently as he began unloading her luggage. He wasn't at all into horses and was amused by Eleanor's obsession with ponies. "Here you go." He tossed her the bag containing her riding equipment.

"Thanks!" Eleanor caught it deftly and walked through the front gate just as the cottage door opened and her aunt came out.

"Eleanor! It's great to see you!" Pippa Treacy gave her niece a hug. She was a tall, slim woman with curly brown hair. Her eyes looked very blue in her tanned face.

"Hi, Aunt Pippa!" Eleanor returned the hug. "I love your new cottage!"

"Me too. I can't believe that I've been here for six months already. You're

my first overnight guest." Pippa was
Eleanor's mom's older sister. She was a
photographer and made her living taking
pictures of wildlife.

"How's the work going for your
exhibit?" Mrs. Gale asked.

"Don't ask!" Pippa sighed, tucking a
strand of hair behind one ear. "I've got so
much to do. I can't believe I'm ever going
to be ready."

"Well, maybe Eleanor will be able
to give you a hand with something,"
Mrs. Gale suggested. "She's pretty good
with a computer."

"Um . . . yeah," Eleanor said,
distracted. All she could think about was
being allowed to ride her aunt's ponies
soon. She was desperately going to miss
her favorite pony, Patch, who she rode at

riding school on the weekends, but being able to ride here every day definitely made up for it! She wondered if she would have a favorite at the end of her vacation—it would be like having her very own pony!

"I'm really sorry that we don't have time to come inside, but we're already running late," her mom said, hugging her sister. "I promise that we'll stay with you for the whole day when we come to pick up Eleanor."

"That would be great!" Pippa said, smiling. "Well—you'd better get going or you'll miss your plane. Have a good trip. And don't worry about Eleanor. We'll be fine, won't we, honey?"

Eleanor nodded at her aunt, kissed her mom and dad good-bye, and then stood

beside Pippa to wave to them as they
drove off. She suddenly felt really sad at
the thought of not seeing them for six
weeks.

As soon as her parents' car was out of
sight, Aunt Pippa took Eleanor into the
cottage and showed her to her bedroom.
It was a pretty, sunny room at the back of
the house. From the window was a view

of the neat back garden, which had a gate
that opened directly onto the forest.

Eleanor noticed that there didn't
seem to be a paddock or any barns.
She wondered where her aunt kept her
ponies.

Wow! This place is pony paradise, she
thought, looking at the pathways that
wound through the enormous trees and
clearings of purple heather and scrubby
grass. Sun shone through the trees and
glinted on a little stream off to one side.
She imagined all the wonderful rides
she'd have.

"Can we go and see your ponies
now?" Eleanor burst out, unable to
control her excitement any longer. "Are
they at a farm or stables? How many do
you have? What are their names?"

Her aunt laughed. "Slow down, Eleanor! One question at a time! I have three: Mary, Jed, and Blue. But going to see them is easier said than done. Free-ranging ponies can wander for long distances. It can take ages to track them down."

Eleanor frowned. What did her aunt mean about her ponies being free-ranging? "But I thought you owned them."

"I do, but it's not quite that straightforward," Pippa explained. "I'm what's called a commoner. That's someone who lives in a house in the forest and who has certain rights—like the right to graze ponies in the forest. My ponies are wild and pretty much take care of themselves in the summer. They have a job to do: looking after the forest."

Eleanor was fascinated. She had never heard of a commoner before. "Are there lots of wild ponies living in the forest and looking after it?"

"About four thousand. They're all owned by other commoners. We give them hay in the winter, pay for health checks, make sure they wear fluorescent collars to keep them safe at night, and so on. There are regular roundups, too, when the herds are thinned out and some of the ponies are sold."

"But how do you find them when you want to ride them?" Eleanor asked eagerly.

Aunt Pippa looked surprised. "I *don't* ride them. None of my ponies are broken in. I'm thinking of buying one to ride

eventually, but it's just another thing I
haven't gotten around to."

"Oh, okay." Eleanor didn't know
what to say. She wouldn't be able to do
any riding this vacation at all! Eleanor
began to miss her mom and dad even
more and wondered whether she should
have gone with them on tour after all.

She tried hard not to let her aunt see

how disappointed she felt. "Well, I guess it could be fun going out on a pony hunt to find Mary, Jed, and Blue," Eleanor said with forced brightness.

"They are really quite special," Aunt Pippa said, smiling. "That's why I love to photograph them. I go out looking for the ponies whenever I get the chance. Even if I can't find them there are usually others around."

Eleanor cheered up a bit at the prospect of meeting her first-ever wild pony. "I'll go and change my shoes before we go into the forest! I'll be right back!" she said eagerly.

Pippa laughed. "Whoa there, young lady! I didn't mean we could go right this minute. I'm afraid I have to head into town now to collect some prints I've had

framed and organize the invitations.
We can go out searching for ponies
tomorrow or the day after. Why don't
you come along with me for the ride?
You could explore the local stores while
I'm at the framer."

Eleanor didn't really feel like
shopping. "I think I'll stay here and
unpack, if that's okay."

"Fine by me. But are you sure you'll
be all right by yourself?"

"Positive. I'm nearly ten now, Aunt
Pippa. I'll sit and read in the garden
when I'm finished."

Pippa beamed at her. "Goodness me!
How grown up you are. Okay then, I
won't be long. I'll bring us something
nice back for dinner. How about pizza?"

Eleanor nodded. "Sounds good."

Her aunt went downstairs. Eleanor heard a car start up and drive off. She sank glumly onto the pretty patchwork quilt that covered her bed and allowed the disappointment to wash over her.

With no ponies to ride, it looked like this was going to be a very lonely summer. Aunt Pippa was lovely, but it was obvious she was going to be really busy getting ready for her exhibit over the next few days. Eleanor tried hard not to wish that she hadn't come. There wasn't even anyone her own age to hang out with.

She got up and put her riding boots and hat in the closet since it didn't look as if she'd have much use for them. After piling the rest of her clothes into the chest of drawers, she picked up her book and went back downstairs.

Eleanor wandered slowly outside into the garden. She went and sat on the lawn for a while, enjoying the warm smell of newly cut grass. Midafternoon sun tipped the tops of the trees with dusty gold light. A robin hopped onto a fence post, looking at Eleanor with its head to one side. It flew off as she put down her book, got up, and walked to the edge of the garden.

Resting her arms on the low garden gate, Eleanor stood staring across the forest clearing. Beyond the patches of heather and dusty-looking grass, she could see a rough path leading into a grove of birch, ash, and oak. She wondered if her aunt's ponies might be somewhere in those trees, watching her with shy, wary eyes.

Suddenly, a sparkling rainbow mist filled the entire clearing, and Eleanor saw rainbow droplets forming and twinkling on her skin.

"Oh!" Eleanor squinted to try to see through the strange mist.

As it slowly cleared, Eleanor noticed that a pony had stepped out of the forest

and was walking slowly toward her. It
had a glossy chestnut coat, a sandy mane
and tail, and large, deep-violet eyes.

"Can you help me, please?" it asked in
a velvety whinny.

Chapter TWO

Eleanor's jaw dropped as she stared at the pony in utter amazement. She hadn't ever seen a real wild pony before, but she was certain that ponies couldn't talk. She shook her head. She must be imagining things.

She clicked her teeth encouragingly. "Hello there. Aren't you gorgeous? I bet you've come to see if Aunt Pippa has an

apple for you. I wonder which one you are: Mary, Jed, or Blue."

The pony's ears flickered, and it lifted its head proudly. "I am neither of those. I am Comet of the Lightning Herd. I have just arrived here from Rainbow Mist Island."

"Y-you really c-can talk?" Eleanor stuttered. "How come?"

"All the magical Lightning Horses in my herd can talk. What is your name?" Comet asked.

"I-I'm Eleanor. Eleanor Gale," she found herself saying. "I'm staying here with my aunt for my summer break." She felt like pinching herself to make sure she wasn't dreaming. But Comet still stood there, looking at her calmly. She noticed again his large bright violet eyes.

Comet dipped his head in a formal bow, and his sandy mane swung forward. "I am honored to meet you, Eleanor."

"Um . . . me too." Eleanor still couldn't quite believe that this was happening, but her curiosity was starting to overtake her shock. Despite being wild, this magical pony didn't seem to be at all nervous around her. "But why are you here in the forest?" she asked.

"I am looking for my twin sister, who is lost and in hiding," Comet told her. "She is called Destiny."

"That's a lovely name. But who is she hiding from?" Eleanor asked, puzzled.

Comet's large eyes glistened with sadness. "We were playing our favorite game of cloud-racing in the night sky when Destiny accidentally lost the Lightning Herd's Stone of Power. I found the stone, but Destiny thought it was gone forever and imagined she was in a lot of trouble, so she ran away. The stone showed me that she is here, in your world. I must find her before she is discovered by the powerful dark horses who want to steal our magic."

Eleanor frowned as she tried to take this in. It all sounded so strange and unreal—like a fairy tale. "You say you and Destiny were *cloud-racing*? But how . . ."

"Please, stand back," Comet ordered, backing away.

Eleanor felt a strange warm prickling sensation flow to the tips of her fingers as violet-colored sparkles blossomed in Comet's chestnut coat, and a light rainbow mist swirled around him. The sturdy forest pony disappeared, and in its place stood a handsome cream-colored pony with a flowing golden mane and tail. Magnificent golden wings covered with gleaming feathers sprung from his shoulders.

Eleanor was speechless with wonder. She had never seen anything so beautiful in her whole life.

"Comet?" she gulped when she could finally speak.

"Yes, it is still me, Eleanor. Do not be afraid." Comet gave a deep musical neigh. There was a final swirl of sparkling mist, and Comet reappeared as the sturdy chestnut pony.

"Wow! That's an amazing disguise!

No one would ever know that you're not an ordinary forest pony," Eleanor said.

"Destiny, too, will be in disguise. But that will not save her if the dark horses discover her," Comet said gravely. "Now I must look for her. Will you help me?"

Eleanor felt a second of doubt at the thought of the dangerous dark horses who were pursuing Comet's twin sister. But then the magic pony leaned forward and pushed his satiny nose into her hand.

Eleanor's soft heart melted as Comet huffed warm breath onto her fingers. "Of course I will!" she said. "We'll search for Destiny together."

"Thank you, Eleanor."

"I can't wait to tell Aunt Pippa about you! She'll be so—"

Comet lifted his head. "No! You must tell no one about me or what I have told you!"

Eleanor felt disappointed that she couldn't confide in her aunt. She felt sure that Aunt Pippa could be trusted.

"You must promise," Comet insisted, blinking at her with his intelligent, deep-violet eyes.

Eleanor nodded slowly. If it would help to keep Destiny safe until Comet could find her and return to Rainbow Mist Island, she was prepared to agree. "Okay. I promise. Cross my heart."

"Thank you, Eleanor."

"But where shall we start looking?" she asked. "There are thousands of ponies in the forest. If Destiny's hiding among them, it'll be almost impossible to find her."

As Comet looked thoughtful, there
was the sound of a car pulling into the
driveway.

Eleanor exclaimed, "Aunt Pippa! She's
back. I can't come with you now. She'll
notice I'm gone. I'll have to try to sneak
out later. You'd better hide before she
sees you!"

"Very well." With a swish of his

sandy tail, the chestnut pony turned and galloped into the trees.

"Eleanor? Where are you, honey? I hope you like pepperoni on your pizza!" Aunt Pippa called from the kitchen.

"I love it! Coming!" Eleanor answered.

As she went back inside, she bit back a huge grin. It looked like her rather lonely summer had just taken a turn for the better. Never in her wildest dreams had she expected to make friends with a magic pony!

Chapter
THREE

Eleanor's heart beat fast as she peeped into the living room where Aunt Pippa was lying on the sofa, taking a short nap after dinner. All was silent, and then she heard a faint snore.

Smiling to herself, Eleanor tiptoed into the kitchen. She was already wearing her jeans and a long-sleeved top, and she sat on the back doorstep to pull on her riding boots and hat. She felt tense with excitement. Would Comet still be there? Or would he have galloped off alone to look for Destiny?

As Eleanor walked through the gate at the bottom of the back garden, the chestnut pony stepped out of the trees, and a warm orange sunset glowed behind him.

"You're still here! I'm so glad," Eleanor exclaimed.

Comet bent his neck to bump his nose very gently against her arm. "Greetings, Eleanor. Climb onto my back. We must go."

Eleanor scrambled onto the chestnut pony. She wasn't used to riding bareback, but the moment she sat astride Comet she felt perfectly at ease. His magic seemed

to spread over her, making her feel warm
and safe.

She twined her hands in Comet's
thick sandy mane as he leaped forward
and galloped into the forest. Huge oak
trees spread their branches overhead as
they followed bridleways and paths. They
came to a picnic area with a closed café
and sped past, pushing deeper into the

forest. There was no one around. Most visitors had left to go home by now.

Eleanor and Comet weaved along twisting paths and tracks. In the warm glow of the setting sun they came upon small herds of ponies, grouped together in clearings or standing under the trees. Each time, Comet paused and trotted up to them, snorting a greeting, but did not find Destiny among any of the ponies.

Comet galloped on tirelessly, his hooves skimming the ground. Eleanor crouched low on his back, feeling the breeze rush by, her hair streaming behind her. She was breathless with the thrill of riding the magic pony.

"Hold tight!" Comet told her as he surged up a hill topped by birch trees.

He paused at the top where the
ground fell away into a deep ravine and
a waterfall foamed into a river far below.
From their position on the high ground,
Eleanor could see the forest spreading out
in all directions—its hundreds of acres
of trees, divided by paths, clearings, and
roads used by tourists and visitors.

"The forest is never-ending," Eleanor

said. "How will we ever find Destiny?"

Comet had stretched his neck and was peering around with his keen eyes. "Because we are twins, we have always had a special bond. If Destiny is close, I will sense her presence. Also, if she has passed by at any time she will have left a trail."

"A trail? What will it look like?" Eleanor asked.

"There will be softly glowing hoofprints, which are invisible to most people in this world."

"Will I be able to see them?" Eleanor asked.

"Yes. If you are riding me or if I am very close to you," Comet told her. "Are you ready, Eleanor? We must keep searching."

"I'm ready!"

Comet sprang forward. He was
wonderful to ride—so smooth, fast, and
exciting. Eleanor kept a close lookout but
she saw no sign of any magical hoof prints,
and although they met other wild ponies,
none of them was Destiny.

Despite the thrill of riding Comet,
Eleanor felt her eyes drooping, and she bit
back a yawn. The sun was now very low
in the sky. Eleanor knew that Aunt Pippa
might wake at any moment.

"You are tired, Eleanor," Comet said
with concern. "I will take you back now."

Back in the clearing outside her aunt's
garden gate, Comet stopped and let
Eleanor slide off his back.

The pony's chestnut head drooped a

little. Eleanor guessed that Comet was missing his twin sister.

"We'll find Destiny," she said, gazing into his large sad eyes, which were as beautiful as amethysts. "I promise I'll do all I can to help."

"Thank you, Eleanor," Comet said gratefully. "I will see you very soon."

With a flick of his tail, he whirled around and melted into the trees.

Eleanor crept into the house and went swiftly upstairs. She took off her riding boots and hat, and heard her aunt stirring. She stood at the top of the stairs just as Pippa came out into the hall.

"My goodness! I must have dozed off. I think I'm ready for bed," Pippa said, hiding a yawn behind her hand.

"Me too. Good night, Aunt Pippa. See you in the morning!" she called.

Tired, but with her thoughts still full of the thrilling forest ride, she went to her room, undressed, and crawled into bed. Moments later, she was fast asleep.

Eleanor woke to find bright yellow light flooding into her room. She threw back the patchwork quilt, her mind buzzing with all that had happened the day before. She looked out her window toward the forest, wondering where Comet was and what he was doing. She could see no sign of him and didn't dare call out in case her aunt heard. Dressing quickly, Eleanor hurried downstairs.

Aunt Pippa was in the kitchen making breakfast. "Good morning, honey. Sleep well?" she asked.

"Yes, fine, thanks," Eleanor said, helping herself to toast and scrambled eggs. All she could think about was going into the forest to find Comet, but she needed to think of a reason for going off by herself. Aunt Pippa wasn't just going to let her wander off without knowing exactly where she was going.

Eleanor puzzled over the problem as
she nibbled a corner of toast. She was starting
to think that it was all hopeless and that
yesterday might even be the only time she
would see Comet when the telephone in the
hall rang.

Aunt Pippa went to answer it and
returned looking a little flustered.

"That was the gallery. They're short-

staffed because someone is sick and
wondered if I'd mind going in and hanging
my photographs," she explained. "I think
I'm going to have to go over there. I'm
sorry, Eleanor. It's going to be boring
for you to come with me and sit around
waiting."

"Why don't I stay here? Then you won't
have to worry about me," Eleanor said
helpfully, trying not to sound too eager. "I
want to finish my book, anyway."

Aunt Pippa looked relieved. "Well,
okay. I hope I'll only be a couple of hours.
Maybe we could go out and look for Mary,
Jed, and Blue after lunch?"

Eleanor nodded, smiling. "I'd like
that."

As soon as she'd said good-bye to her
aunt, Eleanor hurried upstairs to grab her

riding boots and hat and ran out the back
garden gate. She stood in the clearing, her
pulse quickening with excitement as she
faced the trees and called Comet's name.

For a moment, nothing happened
and she almost wondered if yesterday's
thrilling ride had been a dream. But then
the chestnut pony appeared out of nowhere
and walked toward her. His sandy mane
and tail stirred in the breeze.

"Greetings, Eleanor."

"Comet!" Eleanor's heart lifted as she looked at him, thinking how amazing it was that he had chosen her to be his friend. Comet was her own special secret that she would never, ever tell anyone. "I've got two hours to myself. We can go looking for Destiny again!" she cried.

Comet pawed at the ground, his deep-violet eyes flashing with eagerness. "Thank you, Eleanor. Climb onto my back."

Chapter FOUR

Comet set off in a different direction from the one they had taken yesterday. As they galloped between the trees, Eleanor leaned forward and entwined her hands in the pony's thick mane again. Comet moved so smoothly that she felt like a part of him and hardly even needed to grip his sides with her legs.

It suddenly occurred to Eleanor that

she shouldn't ride Comet bareback and
without a head collar in broad daylight.
They hadn't met any other riders yet,
but when they did she was sure to attract
attention.

Comet's ears twitched back as if he
felt her hesitation, and he came to a halt
beneath a large oak tree. "Is something
wrong, Eleanor?"

"It's just that in this world ponies
usually wear saddles and bridles when
they're being ridden," she told him.

Comet listened carefully as she
described the equipment in detail. When
she had finished, he nodded. "I did not
know this. No one has ever ridden me
before. I will see to it now."

Eleanor climbed down from Comet
and stood watching him curiously.

She felt a strange warm tingling sensation in her fingertips as bright violet sparks ignited in Comet's chestnut coat. His ears and tail crackled with tiny lightning bolts of magical power.

Eleanor's eyes widened. Something very strange was happening. She watched in complete astonishment as with a whooshing noise thousands of tiny glittery lights like busy worker bees sprang into the air. The sparkling crowd weaved back and forth. *Crackle! Rustle! Clink!* The lights created a full set of tack just as she'd described it.

"Wow!" Eleanor said breathlessly. Seconds later, Comet stood there fully saddled up.

"Is this right, Eleanor?" Comet asked as the sparks faded from his chestnut coat.

"It's just perfect!" Eleanor adjusted
the girth and slipped two fingers under
the strap to make sure it was firm but
not too tight around Comet's middle.
She mounted, checked her stirrup length,
picked up the reins, and they set off again.

Eleanor and Comet rode along
narrow pathways bordered by birch trees.

Gradually the trees grew thicker and
shadowed the forest floor. They rounded
some bushes and came to a clearing
where a herd of about ten wild ponies
were gathered.

"Oh look. There are some young
ones with them. Aren't they gorgeous?"
Eleanor sighed.

Comet slowed to a walking pace. He
gave a friendly nicker as he moved toward
the rather nervous-looking ponies. They

turned their heads to look at him, their
ears twitching with curiosity.

Suddenly a dog came out of nowhere
and shot straight past them. Barking
loudly, it ran toward the herd. One of
the young wild ponies reared up, its eyes
rolling in terror.

"Bad dog! Get away from them!"
Eleanor shouted. She twisted around to
see if an owner was visible, but there was
no one in sight.

The wild ponies stamped around,
blowing in alarm. The youngsters seemed
ready to bolt in all directions at any
moment. Eleanor was worried that they'd
hurt themselves if they ran off in a blind
panic.

"We'd better scare that dog off before
those ponies scatter!" she cried.

Eleanor was about to squeeze Comet
gently and urge him forward when he
tossed his head nervously and backed up.
She realized that he was also scared of the
dog. Perhaps they didn't have them on
Rainbow Mist Island.

"It's okay, Comet. I'll deal with
this," she said, quickly dismounting and
running toward the dog. But now that
she was closer to it, it seemed a lot bigger
and fiercer.

"Go away! Go on!" she cried, waving
her arms.

The dog turned and looked at her,
and a growl rumbled in its throat. It
started to walk toward her. Eleanor
gulped and began to back up slowly,
regretting her rash decision to face the
dog alone.

She felt another prickling sensation
in her fingertips. It was a lot softer than
last time.

She glanced at Comet and watched
as the chestnut pony opened his mouth
and huffed out a big breath, which turned
into a miniature violet fireball. It shot

toward the dog, trailing bright sparks,
and hit it harmlessly on the nose before
dissolving into a puff of smoke. *Poof!*

"Yip!" The dog gave a surprised yelp
and dashed headlong for the trees with its
tail between its legs.

Eleanor let out a sigh of relief. She
walked back to Comet and patted his silky
neck. "Well done. That showed him! I
was scared for a minute there."

"It was very brave of you to try to
scare that creature away. Thank you,
Eleanor."

"I didn't really think about it. I knew
you were scared and wanted to help. I'd
hate for anything to happen to you," she
said fondly.

Comet nuzzled her arm and she
breathed in his sweet apple-scented breath.

"Hey! What do you think you're doing, letting your dog scare my herd like that!" called an angry voice.

Eleanor looked up to see a girl coming toward them on a bay pony with a white star on its forehead. She looked about twelve years old and was frowning fiercely. Luckily, she seemed to have missed Comet's magic display.

"It wasn't my—" Eleanor began.

But the girl was too angry to listen. "Not your fault, huh? Don't you know the forest code? All dogs have to be kept on leashes!"

"I know. I've seen the signs. I was trying to tell you that it wasn't my dog!" Eleanor said patiently. She mounted Comet so she could explain to the girl properly from up on her horse. "It just came out of nowhere. I don't know who it belongs to, but Comet scared it off because the ponies were about to bolt."

"Oh, I didn't realize." The girl's face cleared and she looked embarrassed. "It was good of you to get him to do that. Sorry, I tend to speak first and think later."

"That's okay. It was an easy mistake," Eleanor said generously.

"Nice of you to say so. You could easily have chewed my head off about it!"

"I'm not that hungry!" Eleanor joked.

They both laughed.

The girl introduced herself. "I'm Francine Boyd, but everyone calls me Frankie. That's a gorgeous pony you've got there. Is he forest-bred?"

"Um . . . yeah. Comet's pretty special," Eleanor said, smiling to herself. *If only*

Frankie knew how much! "I'm Eleanor
Gale. I'm staying at Oak Cottage with
my Aunt Pippa for the summer," she said,
changing the subject quickly and hoping
to avoid any more awkward questions.

Frankie nodded. "I thought I hadn't
seen you around here before. Your aunt's
a photographer, isn't she? Dad said that

a woman who takes incredible photos
of the forest ponies had moved into the
empty cottage."

"That's right. Aunt Pippa's got an
exhibit in town next week," Eleanor said,
smiling at Frankie.

Now that the misunderstanding had
been cleared up, the older girl seemed
really friendly. Eleanor hoped Frankie
might be someone she could get to know
better. It was wonderful having Comet as
a friend, but it would be extra fun having
a pony-crazy friend!

Frankie returned her smile. "I was
just going to have my lunch. Would you
like to share it with me?" she offered. "It's
such a nice day that I brought a picnic
with me. I often do when I'm out with
Jake, checking on our ponies. There's a

pretty stream near here. The ponies can have a drink while we sit and eat."

"Sounds great, thanks!" Eleanor said delightedly. "Is that okay with you?" she whispered to Comet so that Frankie couldn't hear.

Comet nickered an agreement. "I would like to stop for a while."

As Frankie moved forward on Jake, Comet pricked his ears and followed. Eleanor reached forward to pat his silky neck.

"I'm glad we met Frankie," she whispered.

"Me too. I like her," Comet neighed enthusiastically.

Eleanor looked up in alarm to see if Frankie had heard him speak.

Comet seemed to know what she

was thinking. "Do not worry, Eleanor. Only you can hear what I am saying. To anyone else it sounds like a neigh or a snort."

"Oh, okay. Good to know," Eleanor whispered back, hiding a grin.

Comet was full of surprises. She wondered what else he could do.

Sunlight slanted through the trees and made dancing yellow coins of light on the grass path as Eleanor, Comet, Frankie, and Jake rode along together. Eleanor felt a stir of happiness. There was nothing better in the whole world than to be out riding on such a glorious morning— especially on a magic pony!

Chapter
FIVE

Eleanor felt pleasantly full as she
lay on her stomach in the warm grass.
Frankie's cheese and tomato sandwiches
and chocolate brownies washed down
with apple juice had been delicious.

It was beautiful in the grove under
the spreading beech trees, with the stream
bubbling over rocks some distance away.
After a long drink of cool water, Comet

was nibbling a patch of sweet grass a few
feet away. Frankie's pony, Jake, stood
beneath a tree, dozing in the shade.

Eleanor had just finished telling
Frankie about her aunt's three ponies.
"They're called Mary, Jed, and Blue.
We're going out looking for them after
lunch. I hope we get to see them."

Frankie laughed. "Well, don't hold
your breath! Forest ponies can wander

off and be gone for weeks and then just
when you think you'll never see them again,
they'll start hanging around at the end of
your road for ages. It's a good thing your
aunt's got Comet, too, so you can ride him
while you're staying with her. I'd hate it if I
couldn't ride."

"Me too. It's what I love doing the
most," Eleanor said. She thought it was best
to let Frankie assume that Comet belonged
to Aunt Pippa; otherwise she didn't know
how she was going to explain him. "How
many ponies do you own?"

"We've got fifty at the moment. I
won't tell you all their names, you'll never
remember them!" Frankie said, grinning.

"Fifty!" Eleanor echoed. "How do you
keep track of them all?"

"It takes practice, but I'm used to

it. We've always had forest ponies.
Our family has been commoners
for generations. Dad's great-great-
grandmother had six mares. All our
ponies are descended from those."

"Wow! That must have been a
really long time ago." Eleanor was very
impressed. She'd love to live in the forest
and work among the ponies like Frankie
and her family. It would be her dream job
when she grew up.

Eleanor glanced at her watch.

"Oh gosh! Look at the time. I've been
gone for a long time. Aunt Pippa will be
wondering where I am. I'd better go!"

"You can blame me for making you
late by inviting you to lunch, if you'd
like!" Frankie said cheerfully. "It's the
least I could do after blaming you for that

loose dog. Why don't I ride back to Oak Cottage with you? I can explain everything to your aunt."

Eleanor was tempted. She was eager to spend more time with this friendly girl and her pony, but she could hardly ride up to her aunt's house on Comet. She imagined trying to explain to her astonished aunt how she came to be riding a fully tacked-up pony.

"Thanks, but I'll be fine," Eleanor said, hoping that with luck she and Comet might even beat Aunt Pippa back to the cottage.

"Okay then, but if your aunt gets mad at you, tell her to call me!" Frankie gave Eleanor her number. "Are you busy tomorrow? I could show you around the forest tomorrow morning if you'd like. I know all the best rides."

"I'd love that," Eleanor said, mounting Comet. "Bye for now!" she called as he broke into a trot.

"Bye!" Frankie called after them.

Comet had no trouble finding his way back. He stopped in a clump of trees just out of sight of the cottage to let Eleanor dismount. The moment her feet touched the ground, the tack disappeared in a small shower of sparks.

"It's too bad you can't make yourself invisible or something, then you wouldn't have to hide in the forest. You could stay here in the back garden, and I'd be able to sneak out and see you all the time," Eleanor suggested.

Comet blinked his intelligent violet eyes. "That is an interesting idea. I will try out these new powers. I am not yet sure about all the things I can do in this world," he mused.

Eleanor felt a surge of affection for the chestnut pony. She reached up and gave him a swift hug. "Maybe we'll find out more about your magical powers together?"

Comet twitched his ears. "Yes, Eleanor. I think we will."

Eleanor lowered her arms and stood back. "I'd better go. I'll come out to you again soon, and we can look for Destiny again," she promised.

"Very well." Comet tossed his mane and sped away.

Eleanor watched him until he was out of sight and then walked out into the open. She was opening the garden gate when her aunt came out of the kitchen.

"Oh, there you are, Eleanor. I hope you haven't been too bored," Pippa said.

Eleanor smiled. "I've been fine. I had a great time . . . um, exploring." *If my aunt only knew!*

Pippa suddenly looked at her in astonishment. "Why on earth are you wearing your riding gear?"

Eleanor could have kicked herself. She'd completely forgotten about the boots and hat! She thought quickly. "I was . . . um, in the garden when Frankie Boyd came past on Jake," she said, improvising like crazy. "We were talking about her family's ponies and stuff. She offered to let me ride one of them. So I ran inside to get my gear, while she went to get the pony. We didn't go far, just for a short ride."

Her aunt smiled. "I'm glad you met Frankie—you were safe enough in the forest with her. The Boyds are well respected around here. It sounds like you had a good time. I'm glad the two of you got along well. Especially since I ended up taking longer than I'd meant to."

Pippa shook her head slowly. "I'm starting to think that I should postpone this exhibit until after you've gone home. It's not fair for you to have to spend so much time by yourself."

"I don't mind!" Eleanor said quickly, sensing an opportunity. "Besides, I don't have to, now that I've met Frankie. We're going to hang out again tomorrow."

"It sounds like you and Frankie have things all figured out," Pippa said, smiling.

"We do!" Eleanor replied spiritedly.

Pippa put her arm around Eleanor's shoulders, and they went into the cottage together. "To be honest, I'm relieved. I was starting to worry that you'd get bored and wish you hadn't come to stay after all."

"I wouldn't think that, Aunt Pippa. I love being here with you!" Eleanor assured

her truthfully. She didn't mind at all that her aunt was so busy. It meant she could spend lots of time with her new, magical friend.

"I'm very glad about that," Pippa said, smiling fondly. She handed Eleanor a paper bag, which Eleanor hadn't noticed until now. "I was passing a bookstore and thought you might like this."

Eleanor opened the bag and took out a book. "*Big Book of Horses and Ponies of the World*," she read. "Thanks so much. I love it!"

"Time for lunch, I think," Pippa announced. "And didn't I promise that we could go out and look for Mary, Jed, and Blue this afternoon?"

Eleanor beamed at her aunt, wondering how she was going to eat a second lunch. "I can't wait!"

Chapter
SIX

Eleanor spent a happy afternoon
roaming in the forest with her aunt.
They seemed to walk for miles. They
often saw glimpses of ponies through the
trees, and Pippa took a few photographs.
Predictably, there was no sign of Jed,
Blue, or Mary.

That evening, Aunt Pippa cooked a
special dinner. Eleanor was allowed to

help make an apple pie, which made her
feel very grown up.

She slipped out into the garden to
speak to Comet before she went to bed,
but he didn't answer her call. Eleanor
guessed he was deep in the forest looking
for Destiny and couldn't hear her.

That night she had a vivid dream. In
it she saw Destiny disguised as a forest
pony, galloping along one of the winding
trails. Comet's twin sister leaped across
a stream and left a single glowing, violet
hoofprint in the soft mud. Eleanor awoke
abruptly with the strangest feeling that
her dream was true. She decided she
would tell Comet tomorrow morning.

The next day Eleanor got up early.
After breakfast she said good-bye to her

aunt. "I'm off to meet Frankie. See you later!"

"Have a good time!" Pippa called, waving.

Eleanor walked a little into the forest and called to Comet. She planned to ride him out of sight of the cottage to meet up with Frankie where they'd parted yesterday.

Comet stepped out of the trees and snorted and tossed his mane.

"Hello, Comet!" she greeted him warmly. She noticed some small patches of dried mud on his side. Picking a large handful of sweet dried grass, she began brushing him down. "I came out to see you last night before I went to bed, but you were gone. Were you looking for Destiny?"

Comet nodded. "I searched for a long time."

"Did you find any signs of her?" Eleanor asked him.

Comet shook his head sadly. "I saw many more ponies, but Destiny was not with them. And I did not find any glowing hoofprints to show that she had passed by."

"But I think I did!" Eleanor said excitedly. "I saw Destiny in a dream. She left a glowing hoofprint in the mud near a stream. It's almost like Destiny sent me a message in my sleep!"

Comet's bright violet eyes lit up with fresh hope as he reached around to nuzzle Eleanor's arm. "Perhaps she did. It would be just like her!"

Eleanor smiled, pleased to see that he looked less sad. "We can keep a lookout for her today while we're out with Frankie and Jake." She flicked the last traces of mud away and then threw the grass down. "There, finished."

"Thank you, Eleanor."

She felt a familiar tingling down her spine as deep-violet sparkles glimmered once again in Comet's chestnut coat. When they faded, he was fully tacked up, like last time. Eleanor mounted and they set off at a canter.

They were just in time. Frankie and Jake were riding toward them through the trees.

"Hi!" The girls greeted each other, while Comet and Jake touched noses— saying hello in pony fashion.

"It looks like Comet and Jake are already friends!" Frankie said, grinning as they set off, riding abreast.

It was fun to ride into the heart of the forest with Frankie and weave through narrow, lesser-known trails without worrying about getting lost. They glimpsed a number of wild ponies, spread out among the trees. "That herd belongs to one of our neighbors, Mr. Toms," Frankie commented.

"How do you know?" Eleanor asked. She was glad for a reason to stop, so that Comet could check if Destiny was one of them.

Frankie explained that you could recognize different commoners' ponies by the way their tails were cut. "See that one?" She pointed to a gray pony that stood with its back to them. Its tail was cut into a series of blunt steps. "All of the Tomses' ponies have their tails trimmed like that."

Comet had been looking around.
"Destiny is not here." He blew air out of
his nostrils sadly.

Eleanor patted his neck as he rode
down a track, which was bordered by
hedges of hawthorn and brambles and
then opened into a long, flat clearing. It
was a clear run that stretched to the edge
of some open fields.

"We can let the ponies have some
fun," Frankie said, urging Jake on.

"Yay!" Eleanor yelled, pressing
Comet into a gallop.

She could sense the magic pony's
enjoyment as he went faster. He was
exciting to ride, and she loved the feeling
of the wind whistling past them.

"That was amazing!" she said when
they had slowed their ponies to a trot.

Frankie smiled. "Wait until you see where we're going next!" She led the way to where there were some fallen logs. "I often come here to practice jumping," she said. "Jake loves it. Watch this."

She pressed her pony on so that Jake sped up and easily cleared the log. Frankie patted the bay pony's neck. "Good boy! Now you!" she urged Eleanor. "Let's see what Comet can do!"

Eleanor clicked her tongue. Comet didn't hesitate. He leaped forward. Three strides, two strides, one stride . . .

Comet soared through the air and landed safely on the other side of the log.

"Way to go! He almost looked like he was flying!" Frankie exclaimed.

Eleanor bit back a grin.

"You were fantastic!" she whispered
to him with her back to Frankie.

"I enjoyed it, too," Comet said.

The ponies took turns going over the
jumps. After a stop for lunch and a chance
for the ponies to have a drink, they went
for a more leisurely ride along the grass

border beside one of the public roads.

As the afternoon wore on, the girls and ponies headed back to Oak Cottage. Eleanor stopped under the cover of the trees to say good-bye to Frankie and Jake. "Thanks so much. We had a wonderful time! Can we meet up again tomorrow?"

"I don't think I can. Some of the commoners are having a roundup," Frankie explained. "It can get a bit hectic, so I'll probably have to give Dad a hand. I know! Why don't you and Comet come and watch? It's pretty exciting. Visitors aren't usually allowed, but you'll be okay with me. I'll talk about it with Dad. It'll be great for you to see so many forest ponies in one place."

"I wouldn't miss it for anything!" Eleanor waved as Frankie rode away.

Chapter
SEVEN

That evening it poured with rain—an
intense downpour that lasted for hours and
cast a dark veil over the forest.

Eleanor was curled up on the squishy
sofa, reading her new horse and pony
book, but she couldn't concentrate because
she was worrying about Comet. She knew
he'd probably found shelter under the trees,
like the other sturdy forest ponies, but

unlike them, he was all alone and missing
Destiny.

Her aunt was working in her office at
the front of the house, so Eleanor decided
to risk going outside to check on Comet.
Grabbing an umbrella, she hurried
through the back garden and entered the
forest clearing.

"Comet," she called softly.

There was no answer. No chestnut
pony stepped out of the trees and came
toward her. She waited a little longer, but
the magic pony still didn't appear.

"Comet? Where are you?" Eleanor
called again. She thought she heard his
voice, but it was very faint, as if it came
from far away.

"I am here . . ."

Where was he? Puzzled, Eleanor went

back into the house. She decided that
she would have to wait until morning
to go out and look for him. She was just
dumping the dripping umbrella into
the stand in the hall when she heard his
gentle whinny again.

"Eleanor. Come closer. I am here . . ."

Comet sounded a tiny bit louder than
before and seemed to be calling from
upstairs. Curious, Eleanor went up to her
bedroom.

She stood in the open doorway and
looked around. She could sense that
something was different, but what? Her
gaze fell on the table next to her bed.
There beneath the lamp stood a little
toy horse with a fluffy chestnut coat, a
pale mane and tail, and sparkling deep-
violet eyes.

As Eleanor watched, the toy horse
shook itself and twitched its tail.

"Comet?" Eleanor gasped. "Is it really
you? That's so cool!"

"I found another way of using my
magic!" Comet told her proudly in a tiny
soft neigh that matched his new size. She
smiled delightedly at her amazing friend.

"Now you can stay in my room whenever
you want and sleep on my bed. I can even
carry you in my shoulder bag and take
you out with me!"

"I did not think of that. It sounds like
it would be fun!" Comet said.

Eleanor picked him up very gently
and sat on the patchwork quilt with him
on her lap. Comet was handsome as a
chestnut pony and very beautiful as his
true golden-winged self—but right now
he was the cutest and fluffiest miniature
pony she had ever seen.

She was so engrossed in admiring
Comet's tiny neat hooves and little
pointed ears that she didn't notice the
bedroom door swing open.

"I thought I heard you come up
here. I was just going to make some

hot chocolate and wondered if . . . my
goodness! What *do* you have there?"
Aunt Pippa exclaimed, her eyes widening.

Eleanor froze in shock, but it was too
late to hide Comet.

"It's . . . um . . . I was just . . . ," she
faltered. Her mind was a total blank.

"What a gorgeous little toy pony!"
Pippa's face softened as she came forward.
"It's perfect in every detail. Did Frankie
give it to you?" she asked.

Aunt Pippa thinks Comet is a toy? Huh?
Eleanor frowned in confusion. She could
feel Comet's heartbeat against her fingers
and see him twitching his ears and tail.
She couldn't believe that her aunt hadn't
noticed.

"Um . . . yeah. It's cute, isn't it?
I'm calling him Comet," she said. "It

was nice of Frankie—I really like her.
She asked me to go out again with her
tomorrow. There's going to be a roundup
of some of the commoners' ponies. She
said that I could go and watch."

"You really are pony-crazy, aren't
you?" Pippa said, looking thoughtful.

"I am! Ponies are the most wonderful

things in the entire universe!" Eleanor
sang out.

Her aunt laughed fondly. "I won't
argue with that!"

Eleanor quickly slipped Comet behind
her back and gently tucked him between
her pillows, just in case her aunt felt like
looking at him more closely.

"You'll enjoy the roundup," Pippa said.
"The Boyd herd has the best pedigree
around here. Their ponies bring in good
prices. There'll be other commoners with
their herds there, too. I think I'll come
with you. It'll be a chance to get some
good photographs."

"Sounds good," Eleanor said, so
relieved by the change of subject that she
wasn't really concentrating. As soon as her
aunt had gone downstairs to make the hot

chocolate, she turned to Comet. "Phew! I was so worried when she came in. What just happened? I don't get it."

"I used my magic again, so that only you can see me move and hear me speak," Comet said. "Anyone else will think that I am just a fluffy toy."

"I never know what to expect with you. I love having you as a friend," Eleanor said, grinning from ear to ear. Suddenly, her face fell. "Uh-oh. Did Aunt Pippa just say that she was coming with us tomorrow to take photos of the ponies during the roundup?"

Comet nodded his tiny head. "I think that she did."

Eleanor groaned. "Oh no!"

So far she had managed to keep Aunt Pippa away from Frankie so that her aunt

wouldn't find out about Comet being
a life-size pony! She chewed her lip as
she wondered what might happen when
Frankie and her aunt talked, as they were
bound to do tomorrow.

What on earth was she going to do?

Chapter EIGHT

"There's nothing else to do. I'm going to have to walk over to meet Frankie and think of some excuse as to why I'm not riding you," Eleanor decided as she fastened her boots the following day. "I just hope that Frankie doesn't start asking Aunt Pippa where *her* pony Comet is. And why I'm not riding him today!"

"Thank you for helping me, Eleanor. I know it has not always been easy for you," Comet said gratefully.

"I wouldn't have it any other way," Eleanor said fondly, stroking the tiny pony's fluffy coat. "It's a shame you have to stay behind, though. There's a good chance that with so many ponies around, you'd find Destiny among them."

"I think so, too. That is why I *am* going to come with you," Comet said.

"But how? You can't do that without giving yourself away." Eleanor stopped as she realized what Comet meant. "Oh, I get it. You're going to use your magic to stay as a fluffy toy? Great idea. I'll get my shoulder bag!"

She found the bag and laid it on the floor with the top open. Comet jumped

inside, lay down, and folded his legs
beneath him.

Downstairs, Aunt Pippa was ready
to go. She was holding her camera. "All
set?" she said, smiling as Eleanor came in
with her bag over her shoulder.

Eleanor nodded.

Pippa smiled warmly. "We'll soon
be able to have lots more days out. My
exhibit's almost up and running now.

I really appreciate how you've been so patient and understanding about having to entertain yourself."

"That's okay. I was never bored," Eleanor said. There was no chance of that with Comet around!

The forest smelled fresh and new. Large drops were dripping from the trees after last night's heavy rain. But the sunshine was already drying the ground as Eleanor, Comet, and Pippa set out to walk toward the roundup area.

"We'll go this way. It's a shortcut," Aunt Pippa said, turning onto a stony track that wound between tall field maples.

They had been walking for about ten minutes when Pippa suddenly stopped.

"Well, look at that," she whispered, pointing to three ponies that were nibbling the short grass. "There's Jed, Blue, and Mary. They always turn up when you least expect it."

Eleanor watched delightedly as her aunt called to her wild ponies. Recognizing her voice, they lifted their heads, ears twitching. As they walked toward Pippa, Eleanor saw they were all wearing their fluorescent collars for night safety.

"It's best if you keep your distance. They know me, but it can be dangerous for a stranger to approach them," Pippa warned.

"They're gorgeous," Eleanor said, admiring her aunt's ponies. Mary was a dark bay with a gentle face, Jed was a lively looking gray with a black tail, and Blue was a sweet little brown pony with black points.

Pippa took some slices of apple and

carrot out of her pocket. "I always have some treats with me," she told Eleanor. Her ponies munched happily for a few moments; then, as Pippa, Eleanor, and Comet walked on, they went back to grazing.

"I'm glad I got to see them at last," Eleanor said.

She and her aunt continued down
the path, which widened and opened
into an oval-shaped clearing ringed with
flowering bushes. Eleanor opened her
shoulder bag so that Comet could look
out as they walked.

Aunt Pippa noticed Comet's tiny
legs, which were looped over the bag's
opening, and smiled. "How sweet. You've
brought Comet with you!" she observed.

Eleanor nodded, smiling. "You're . . .
er, never too old for a cuddly toy."

The sounds of voices and ponies
came toward them through the trees, and
Eleanor knew they must be getting close
to the roundup area.

Suddenly, she did a double take and
stopped dead in her tracks.

Stretching ahead of them and curving

out of sight was a faint line of softly
glowing violet hoofprints.

Eleanor heard Comet's excited voice
from inside her bag. "Destiny! She has
been here!"

Eleanor gasped. Did that mean that
Comet was leaving to go after her? "Can
you tell where she is? Is she somewhere

close?" she whispered to him anxiously.

"No. The trail is cold. But it proves that Destiny came this way. When I am close to where she is, I will be able to hear her hoofbeats. And I may have to leave suddenly . . . without saying good-bye."

"Oh." Eleanor felt a sharp pang as she realized that she would never be ready to lose her magical friend. "I was hoping that once you found Destiny, you might both stay here with me," she said in a small voice.

Comet shook his head. "It is not possible. We have to return to our family on Rainbow Mist Island. I hope you understand, Eleanor?"

Eleanor nodded sadly, and her eyes pricked with tears. She swallowed hard as she decided not to think about Comet

leaving and promised herself instead
that she was going to enjoy every single
moment spent with him.

Up ahead, Aunt Pippa had stopped
to wait for her. "Is something wrong,
honey?" she asked, frowning with concern
at Eleanor's sad face. "No, I'm . . . er,
fine," Eleanor said, making a big effort to
cheer up. "I had a cramp in my side, but
it's gone now."

"Good. We're almost there." Eleanor
hurried to catch up with her aunt. The
sounds of voices, ponies snorting, and
car doors slamming were even louder.
Despite her worries, Eleanor found herself
looking forward to seeing Frankie and
Jake again.

They emerged to one side of a group
of buildings and wooden pens, some of

them already filled with ponies of all ages.
Cars and trucks were parked all around,
and lots of people stood around in groups.
Others were watching their ponies being
treated by vets.

"Hi, Eleanor!"

It was Frankie. She was standing next
to a large pen with a man who looked so
much like her that he had to be her father.

Eleanor waved, grinning, and she and
her aunt began walking toward them.

Just then, two men on horseback
appeared. They were trying to get a herd
of nervous ponies to go into an empty
pen. There was a sudden loud bang as a
car backfired. A large roan pony rolled
its eyes and squealed in fright. It plunged
sideways, avoiding the pen. Other ponies
followed it, blindly galloping after the big

roan in their terror.

The horsemen tried to get the ponies under control. But it was too late. People scattered in all directions as the ponies stampeded.

"Look out!" someone shouted.

Eleanor gasped. The ponies were thundering straight toward her and Aunt Pippa. And Comet couldn't use his magic to save them without giving himself away!

Chapter
NINE

"Quick! Eleanor! Get behind a tree!"
Aunt Pippa shouted to Eleanor.

With only seconds to spare, Eleanor
leaped sideways, but her foot skidded on
a wet leaf and she went sprawling. Her
shoulder bag slipped off, and the toy pony
fell out and rolled over and over, coming
to rest under a bush.

As Eleanor struggled to her feet, she

felt the now-familiar tingling sensation fizz in the tips of her fingers and saw the bush sparkle with pretty violet light.

Time seemed to stand still.

Comet exploded out of the trees. He leaped toward Eleanor, shielding her

with his body as he faced the oncoming ponies. Rearing up onto his hind legs, he whinnied a warning.

The ponies swerved in all directions, pounding past Eleanor and narrowly missing her with their flying hooves. The second they were past, Comet glanced at Eleanor to check that she was unhurt and streaked away into the forest.

Aunt Pippa ran over and helped Eleanor stand up as men on horseback galloped past them in pursuit of the loose ponies.

"Are you hurt?" her aunt asked, white-faced.

"No. I'm fine. Just a bit shaken up," Eleanor said, catching her breath. *Thanks to Comet*, she thought.

"That chestnut pony came out of

nowhere, but I'm very glad it did! It saved you from a nasty injury. I wonder who it belongs to," Aunt Pippa said.

Eleanor didn't answer.

Just then, Frankie ran up, too. "Eleanor! What happened? We couldn't see back there."

"The loose ponies missed me. I'm okay now. The show's over!" Eleanor joked to show that she really was fine. Hoping that everyone would stop fussing, she walked determinedly toward the pony pens. "Come on. I don't want to miss anything!" she called.

They reached the pens just as a man holding a clipboard made an announcement. The pony sale was about to begin. An air of excitement hung over the crowd as the bids started.

Frankie's dad came over to introduce himself. "You must be Eleanor. Frankie's told me about you."

Eleanor smiled at him. "Hi. Pleased to meet you, Mr. Boyd."

Mr. Boyd turned to Aunt Pippa. "I'm a great admirer of your photographs, Ms. Treacy. I look forward to seeing your exhibit."

"Thank you. Nice of you to say so," Pippa said, smiling. "I'm hoping to take a few photographs today . . . among other things," she said mysteriously, looking sideways at Eleanor.

Eleanor frowned, puzzled. What did her aunt have in mind?

But before she could find out, Eleanor heard a sound she had been hoping for and dreading at the same time.

The hollow sound of galloping hooves overhead.

She froze. Destiny! There was no mistake. And if Eleanor could hear her, then Comet must be very close.

Eleanor set off into the forest at a run. "There's something I have to do!" she called over her shoulder.

She raced through the trees. The magical hoofbeats sounded louder and very close now.

As she reached a thick clump of bushes, a twinkling rainbow mist floated down around her. She looked up to see Comet in his true form—a sturdy chestnut pony no longer. Sunlight gleamed on his noble head, magnificent golden wings, and cream coat. His flowing mane and tail sparkled like strands of spun silk.

"Comet!" Eleanor gasped. She had almost forgotten how beautiful he was as a Lightning Horse. "You're leaving right now, aren't you?" she asked, her voice breaking.

Comet's deep-violet eyes lost a little of their twinkle as he smiled sadly. "I must,

if I am to catch Destiny and save her from our enemies."

A heavy wave of sadness washed over Eleanor, but she knew she was going to have to be brave. She ran forward and threw her arms around Comet's shining neck. "I'll never forget you!"

He allowed her to hug him one last time and then gently stepped backward. "Farewell, my young friend. Ride well and true," he said in a deep musical voice.

There was a final violet flash of light, and a silent fountain of rainbow sparkles fell like soft rain around Eleanor, crackling as they hit the ground. Comet spread his wings and soared upward. He faded and was gone.

Eleanor wiped her eyes. Something glittered on the ground. It was a single

shimmering wing-feather. Reaching
down, she picked it up.

It tingled against her palm as it faded
to a cream color. Eleanor tucked the
feather into her pocket. She would always
keep it to remind herself of the wonderful
adventure she and Comet had shared. She
was so proud that the magic pony had
chosen to be her friend.

When Eleanor stepped out of the
trees, Frankie ran up to her. "There you
are. Your aunt's looking for you!"

Eleanor looked over Frankie's
shoulder to where her aunt stood holding
a gorgeous chestnut pony by its head
collar. The pony had a sandy mane and
tail and gentle deep brown eyes. "Come
and meet my new pony, Eleanor. It's
time I bought one to ride, and you can

exercise her whenever you come and stay
with me. I think perhaps you deserve a
pony in your life aside from Comet."

"Wow!" whistled Frankie. "How
lucky are you?"

Eleanor grinned as she realized Frankie

didn't know that her aunt was referring
to what she thought was her niece's toy
pony.

"How would you like to choose her
name?"

Eleanor thought of Comet on his
journey to find his twin sister. She hoped
they were reunited soon. "Thank you
so much, Aunt Pippa. I'd like to call her
Destiny."

Magic Ponies

A Special Wish

SUE BENTLEY

Prologue

Comet tried to squash a small flutter of hope as he flew back toward his magical island home. "Destiny must be home safely by now!" the young magic pony cried. His twin sister had been lost for a long time.

Spreading his gold-feathered wings, he soared downward, speeding across the wide sea and galloping over the crests of the waves. Soon, Rainbow Mist Island came into view. Its mountains and forests were almost hidden in softly shimmering, multicolored clouds that gave the island its name. Comet's heart lifted. It felt good to be home.

The magic pony drifted over the shore. Rainbow droplets gleamed like jewels on his cream coat and flowing golden mane and tail. Moments later, he touched down onto the grass of a small clearing.

Tossing his head, Comet looked about warily at the huge trees that grew all around, their glowing leaves tinkling faintly. He could feel no trace of the dark horses who wanted to steal his magic.

As the magic pony snorted with satisfaction, there was a movement and an older horse with a wise expression stepped forward.

"Blaze!" Comet bent his neck in a bow before the leader of the Lightning Herd. Blaze's dark eyes softened with affection.

"I am pleased to see you again, Comet. But where is Destiny?" he asked in a deep gentle voice.

"She is not here? Then she is still in danger!" Comet whinnied sadly.

Destiny had playfully borrowed the Stone of Power, which protected the Lightning Herd from the dark horses, but the stone was accidentally lost while the twin magic ponies were playing cloud-chase. Comet later found the stone, but before he could tell Destiny, she ran away, thinking she was in lots of trouble.

"My sister still thinks she has put the Lightning Herd in danger and cannot forgive herself," Comet explained to the older horse. A lump rose in his throat as he realized that his twin sister was alone and in hiding far from home.

Blaze shook his wise old head slowly. "You must go after her again, my young friend. Find Destiny and tell her that the Stone of Power is safe and bring her home."

Comet's deep-violet eyes flashed. He lifted his head. "I will leave at once!"

"Wait!" Blaze ordered. Stamping his foot, he pawed at the grass. A fiery opal, swirling with flashes of rainbow light, appeared. "The stone will help you find her."

The magic pony drew closer to the Stone of Power. A tremor passed over his pale silky coat as he peered deeply into the rainbow depths. The stone grew larger and rays of dazzling light spread outward.

An image formed in the center. Comet gasped as he saw Destiny galloping across a green hillside beneath an open blue sky, in a world far away.

"I have to find her!" he whinnied.

There was a bright flash of dazzling violet light, and rainbow mist surrounded Comet. The cream-colored pony, with his flowing golden mane and tail, and gleaming gold-feathered wings, disappeared. In his place there stood an elegant Connemara pony with a dapple-gray coat, a darker gray mane and tail, and glowing deep-violet eyes.

"There is no time to lose. Go now," Blaze urged. "Use this disguise. Find your twin sister and return with her safely."

"I will!" Comet vowed.

The dapple-gray pony's coat ignited with violet sparks. Comet snorted as he felt the power building inside him. The shimmering rainbow mist swirled faster and faster and drew Comet in . . .

Chapter
ONE

Marcie Locket felt her heart beat
faster as she stood in her garden, looking
over the fence into the adjoining field.
There was a big old shed on one side—
perfect for a stable and storeroom. Her
new pony was going to love its paddock!

Marcie beamed as she imagined all
the fun she would have looking after
a pony of her own. It was going to be

wonderful to go out riding whenever she liked. She might even get her dad to help her put a jumping course up in the field.

"Marcie! Where are you?" her mom called impatiently. "We need to go. I'll be waiting for you in the car."

"Coming!" Marcie answered.

Whirling round, she headed up the garden and into the house. The front door slammed shut behind her as she hurried out to the front drive.

"Sorry, Mom!" Bouncing into the front seat, Marcie dumped her school bag on the floor and fastened her seat belt.

"Hmm. I don't need three guesses to know where you've been," Mrs. Locket said, smiling sideways at her as she waited for a gap in the traffic before pulling out. Marcie smiled back, her eyes glowing

with happiness. "When's Dad going
to hear about his job promotion?" she
asked. He had promised that Marcie
could get her pony once his new job was
confirmed.

"I think he should find out by the end
of the day," her mom replied.

"Great! We can start looking at ponies
for sale. It's Friday today, so we've got the
whole weekend," Marcie said excitedly.

But then she sighed as she thought about her best friend who had recently moved away. "I wish Lara was still here. She had tons of pony magazines. We could have looked through them to help me decide what kind of pony I should get."

"You really miss her, don't you? It's a shame she had to move so far away. But you both promised to keep in touch by phone and e-mail, didn't you? And Lara can always come to visit during vacations," Mrs. Locket added.

Marcie knew her mom was right, but at that moment it didn't make her feel much better. It wasn't going to be the same without her best friend living around the corner. Marcie and Lara had known each other since they were in preschool and had always been together as they moved up grades. They used to spend every weekend together, taking turns riding Lara's pony, Tramp.

"Lara's going to forget all about me," Marcie said glumly. "She'll be busy making new friends and riding ponies with them."

"I'm sure she'll remember her old friends, too," her mom chided gently. "And don't forget, there'll be a brand-new reason why Lara will be delighted to come and visit."

"Oh yeah! My new pony!" Marcie exclaimed, starting to cheer up a bit again. "Lara will want to know everything about it, and she'll be dying to ride it."

As they drove through the busy streets, Marcie let her thoughts wander, picturing ponies of every breed and color imaginable. There were so many gorgeous ones out there. Where would they buy hers from? What was she going to call him or her?

They reached the school, and Mom dropped her at the entrance. Marcie gave her a kiss and waved as she drove away. Marcie wandered into school in a daze—all she could think about was her new pony!

When she got to her usual desk by the window, she found Jessica Evans already sitting there. Jessica looked up and smiled as Marcie sat down. "Hi, Marcie. Miss Slater told me to sit here. I'm your new desk-buddy!"

Marcie smiled. "Um . . . hi, Jessica. Fine by me." She didn't mind Jessica at all, but no one could ever replace Lara.

As the rest of the class filed in and took their seats, Jessica began telling Marcie about the new computer game she'd gotten for her birthday.

"It's got an amazing console. I was playing games with my brother all last night and I got a really high score! He was really jealous. What did you do?" she asked.

"I put a bits 'n' bridles poster up in my bedroom. It has all the different types, like snaffle bits and flash nosebands," Marcie began enthusiastically. "I'm getting a pony of my own really soon, so I'm thinking about getting new equipment for it . . ." She stopped as she noticed a glazed expression settle on Jessica's face.

"I just don't get ponies and riding at all," Jessica commented. "I mean, what's the big deal about galloping through muddy fields and stuff and being freezing? Then you have to get up early to clean out smelly, old, messy stables and build muck piles, don't you?"

"Well, yes," Marcie admitted. "But I like the smell of horses, and there's other stuff to do that's lots of fun. It's all part of looking after your pony."

Jessica widened her eyes incredulously. "Fun? I'd rather hang upside down in

Jell-O. I'll stick to my computer games, thanks."

"Okay." Marcie didn't know quite what else to say. A small wave of loneliness washed over her and she realized that she was missing Lara more than ever.

The rest of the day seemed to drag on forever and Marcie was relieved when the bell rang for the end of school. The moment Miss Slater dismissed the class, Marcie grabbed her school bag and raced outside to meet her mom.

"Did Dad text you?" she asked eagerly as they drove home.

Mrs. Locket shook her head. "There's no news yet. You'll have to be patient for once. Although I know that's not your strong point!" she said, laughing.

Marcie grinned. "Impatient? Me?!" When they got home, Marcie ran upstairs to change out of her school clothes. She was just putting on her jeans when she heard the front door. Her dad was home! Dashing out of her room, she shot back down the stairs, two steps at a time.

"Hi, Dad!" Marcie sang, looking up at him excitedly. She stopped; why did he have such a serious look on his face? Today was a good day for all of them!

"Hello, sweetie." Mr. Locket hung up his jacket and then ran his fingers through his short brown hair. "Where's your mom?"

"Um . . . in the kitchen making dinner, I think," Marcie said, starting to feel like something was wrong.

She went and stood next to her mom

as her dad sat down at the table and began speaking. "I'm afraid I have bad news. We were all called into a meeting late this afternoon and told that the company's closing down," he explained. "I'm going to have to find another job. And to be honest, the way things are right now, that could take some time."

"Oh dear. That's quite a shock." Mrs. Locket sank into a kitchen chair next to her husband and took his hand. "Well, we'll manage. We'll just have to make cutbacks," she decided firmly.

Marcie's heart sank. Something as expensive as a pony would definitely be one of the cutbacks her mom was talking about. But she bit her lip as she looked at Dad. He seemed pale and tense, although he was trying hard to put on a brave face.

She felt really bad for him.

Marcie went and gave both of her parents a hug. "I'm really sorry about your job, Dad. And I can wait a bit longer for my pony."

"Thanks, honey. That's my grown-up girl." Her dad hugged her back and dropped a kiss on the top of her head. "And don't you worry. Your mom and I will work this out."

Marcie nodded. She could tell that they had lots to talk about. "I think I'll . . . um . . . go and sit in the garden . . . or something," she said.

Her mom nodded absently.

Marcie went outside and trudged down to the paddock. She sighed as she thought that it could be empty for quite a while. If only Lara was here. Marcie could

have gone over to her house for a long, comforting talk.

Suddenly, there was movement over near the old shed.

Marcie's eyes widened in surprise as

a dapple-gray pony with a darker gray mane and tail appeared from behind it and began walking toward her.

"Can you help me, please?" it asked in a velvety neigh.

Chapter
TWO

"Oh!" Marcie did a double take.

She swallowed hard as she gazed at
the pony in utter astonishment. What was
going on? Had her mom and dad bought
it as a surprise?

But how could they have done that,
when her dad had just lost his job?

Marcie couldn't figure out why there
was a pony in her paddock. And her

imagination was obviously working
overtime, because she'd just imagined
that it had spoken to her!

As the pony leaned forward, Marcie
reached a hand toward it. It had a short
elegant head with a slightly dished nose
and unusually large eyes. They were a
stunning deep-violet color and shone
like amethysts.

She had never seen or heard of any pony with eyes like that before.

"Hello," she breathed softly, letting it snuffle her to get her scent. "You're absolutely gorgeous. You look like a Connemara pony. But how did you get in here?"

"I have just arrived from far away. My name is Comet of the Lightning Herd. What is yours?" asked the pony.

Marcie dropped her hand in shock and took two steps backward. This pony really *had* just spoken to her. This couldn't be happening! Talking ponies only existed in fairy tales!

But the beautiful pony twitched his ears forward and stood looking at her calmly as if waiting for a reply to his question.

"I'm Marcie," she gulped when she could speak again. "Marcie Locket. I live here with my parents."

Comet dipped his head in a bow. "I am honored to meet you, Marcie," he said politely.

"Um . . . me too," Marcie blurted out. She recalled something the pony had just said. "What's . . . the Lightning Herd?"

"We are a family of horses who live on Rainbow Mist Island," Comet told her proudly. "Our leader is wise and strong. He is called Blaze. A Stone of Power protects our herd from the dark horses who would like to steal our magic."

Marcie listened carefully, still having trouble taking all this in.

"So why are you *here*?" she asked him.

Comet gave a soft blow. "My twin sister,

Destiny, lost the Stone of Power when
we were cloud-racing. I found it and it
is safe again, but Destiny does not know
this. She thought she was in terrible
trouble for losing the stone, so she ran
away to hide in your world. I have come
here to look for her."

Marcie's curiosity seemed to be
getting the better of her shock. "You
and your twin sister were *cloud-racing*?
But how . . ."

Comet backed away from the fence.
"I will show you. Stay there," he neighed
gently.

Marcie felt a strange warm tingling
sensation flow to the very tips of her
fingers as violet sparkles bloomed in
Comet's dapple-gray coat and a veil of
shimmering rainbow mist surrounded him.

The gray pony disappeared, and in its place stood a magnificent young cream-colored pony, with a flowing gold mane and tail. Springing from his shoulders were powerful wings, covered with gleaming golden feathers.

"Oh wow!" Marcie gasped, absolutely spellbound. The winged pony was the most beautiful thing she had ever seen. She caught her breath. "C-Comet?"

"Yes, Marcie. It is still me," Comet said in a deep musical whinny.

But before she could get used to the sight of Comet in his true form, there was a final swirl of glittering rainbow mist and Comet reappeared as a handsome dapple-gray Connemara pony.

"That's a really cool disguise! Can Destiny use her magic to disguise herself, too?" Marcie asked.

Comet nodded. "But that will not save her from the dark horses if they discover her. She is in danger. I need to

find her and take her back to the safety of
Rainbow Mist Island. Will you help me,
Marcie?"

Marcie saw that Comet's deep-violet
eyes were shadowed by worry for his sister,
and her heart melted. "Of course I will.
Oh, just wait until I write to my best
friend, Lara, about you."

Comet swished his dark gray tail. "I
am sorry, but you can tell no one about
me and what I have told you!"

Marcie was disappointed. She would
have loved to share this amazing secret
with Lara. It would have been very
special, more than ever with Lara living so
far away now.

"You must promise," Comet said,
looking at her with his big eyes.

Marcie nodded slowly. If it would

help protect his twin sister from the dark horses until Comet could find her, she was prepared to agree. "I promise. No one's going to hear anything about you and Destiny from me."

"Thank you, Marcie."

Reaching forward, Comet gently

bumped his nose against Marcie's arm.
She reached up to pat his satiny cheek.

"Marcie? Are you still down there?"
called a voice. Marcie stiffened as she
looked back at the big flowering bushes
that screened the field from the house.
She caught a glimpse of her mom's bright
blue top through a small gap in the leaves.

"Mom's coming!" she gasped in panic.

Oh no! There wasn't time for her
to hide Comet. Her mom was going to
see her new magical pony friend at any
second! What was she going to do?

Chapter
THREE

"There you are, sweetie," Mrs. Locket said, slipping her arm around Marcie's shoulder as she came and stood beside her at the fence. "I thought I'd find you here, staring at that rickety old shed we were going to turn into a stable. I hope you're not too upset about having to wait for your pony."

"Um . . . well, I am a b-bit disappointed," Marcie stammered. Why didn't her mom say anything about the gorgeous dapple-gray pony that was standing in the field as large as life?! Instead, she was just looking back at her in concern—it was almost as if she couldn't see Comet.

Marcie continued on carefully. "I don't feel all that bad. It's not as if I'm never going to be able to have one, is it?" She was surprised to find that now that Comet had arrived, she really was okay about having to wait for a pony of her own.

"Thanks for being so understanding, Marcie. Your dad's taken it quite hard," Mrs. Locket said. She sighed. "I just hope it won't be too long before he finds work again."

"It won't be. I've got a good feeling about it," Marcie said.

"I hope you're right." Her mom
smiled and reached out to ruffle Marcie's
shoulder-length brown hair. "Well—
dinner's almost ready. I'm just about to
serve it. Are you coming in?"

Marcie looked at Comet, who
was listening to the conversation, his
intelligent eyes twinkling. It was really

··153·*·*

odd. But Mrs. Locket *still* didn't seem to
have noticed him.

"Marcie?"

Marcie's head snapped back. "I'll be
there in a minute."

"All right then." Her mom turned and
went back to the house.

Marcie waited until she was out of sight
behind the bushes before talking to Comet.
"I don't get it. What just happened?"

"I used my magic so that only you can
hear and see me," Comet told her.

"Really?" Marcie was delighted. "So
you're invisible now? That's really cool." She
had a sudden idea. "Why don't you live in
this paddock? No one will know except me.
There's lots of juicy grass to eat, rainwater in
the trough, and the shed for shelter if it rains.
And I'll come and see you whenever I can!"

Comet nodded. "This is a good place to stay while I am searching for Destiny."

"Then it's settled," Marcie said happily. "I'd better go now, or Mom and Dad will wonder what's taking me so long. I'll sneak out to see you later."

"Thank you, Marcie." Comet turned and walked a few steps, then bent his head and began cropping the grass with his strong young teeth.

After a final glance over her shoulder, Marcie hurried back to the house. There was a brand-new pony in her paddock after all! But never in her wildest dreams could she have imagined that it would be one as amazing and magical as Comet!

Marcie was almost too excited to eat, but she made herself take her time. She

didn't want her mom and dad to think
she had a stomachache and make her
take a nap.

After they finished dinner, Marcie
helped load the dishwasher and her mom
insisted she do an hour of homework.
Sighing, she went upstairs to do it all
in double-quick time—she wanted
to spend every minute possible with
Comet!

When Marcie was sure her mom
and dad were engrossed in watching
the news on TV, she decided to risk
sneaking out to see Comet. She grabbed
an apple from the fruit bowl on the
kitchen table and quickly chopped it up
before disappearing into the garden.

The sun was setting, and streaks
of peach and salmon pink colored the

darkening sky. It was a beautiful evening, and as Marcie jogged down the garden to the paddock, her heart began beating fast. She couldn't wait to see the magic pony again. But he wasn't standing in the paddock where she'd left him.

"Comet!" she called.

There was no answer. No handsome dapple-gray pony came galloping up the field. The door of the big old shed hung open. Maybe Comet was inside. Marcie

went into the paddock to look.

But he wasn't in the shed, or behind it, or anywhere else.

Marcie's high spirits took a dent as she wondered whether Comet had changed his mind about staying in the paddock. Maybe he had grown tired of waiting for her and gone to find someone else to help him search for Destiny.

"Comet! Where are you?" she called again, starting to get worried.

There was a faint rustling sound from behind her.

"I am here, Marcie," Comet nickered, blowing warm breath into her hair.

Marcie spun around, a huge grin spreading across her face. He smelled wonderful—of grass and fresh air and something sweet that was his own magical scent. She threw her arms around his neck and pressed her cheek to its silky warmth.

"Oh, I'm so glad you came back!" she burst out. "I thought that maybe you'd left because you didn't like it here."

"I like it very much." Comet's violet eyes glowed with amusement. "I simply went to have a look around while I was waiting for you. There might have been traces of where Destiny has passed by."

Lowering her arms, Marcie stepped back. "What sort of traces?" she asked curiously.

"Wherever Destiny goes, she leaves a trail of softly glowing hoofprints that are invisible to most people in your world," Comet told her, twitching his ears.

"Really?" Marcie said, amazed. "Will I be able to see them?"

Comet nodded. "But only if you are
riding me or I am very close to you."

Marcie knew he must be longing to
find his twin sister, who was all alone
and missing her family. "I should be able
to come and help you look for Destiny
tomorrow. We usually go shopping together
early on Saturdays. Mom and Dad always
take hours, and it can be really boring. I'll
make an excuse to stay here," she decided.

Comet looked pleased. "Thank you,
Marcie."

Marcie remembered the apple in her jeans
pocket. "I brought something for you."

She took the slices out and offered them
to Comet on her flattened palm. The magic
pony stretched forward and she felt his soft
lips nuzzling her cautiously as he picked up
a piece of apple.

He started crunching and in a few
moments he had eaten the whole apple.
"That was delicious. I like your human
food."

"Wait until you try carrots and
peppermints!" Marcie smiled, feeling a
rush of affection for her amazing new
friend. "See you in the morning then.
Sweet dreams," she called to him as she
went toward the gate.

Chapter
FOUR

"Are you sure that you don't want to change your mind and come with us?" Marcie's dad asked the following morning as he picked up his car keys.

"Positive!" Marcie said firmly. "You know I hate food shopping. I thought I'd . . . um . . . send Lara a really long e-mail. I want to know how she's doing at her new school, what her new house is like,

and if there are lots of good places to go out
riding on Tramp."

"Good idea, sweetie. You and Lara can
catch up on all the pony news, like you
used to," her dad said. His face clouded. "I
bet she'll be disappointed to hear that you
won't be getting a new pony after all."

"Maybe at first, but she'll understand, like I do," Marcie said brightly. "Some things are better when you have to wait for them." *Especially when you already have a secret magic pony friend to keep you company!* she thought.

"I'm glad you're able to see things that way," her dad said, looking happier.

"See you later!" Marcie waved as their car drove away and she closed the front door.

She pulled on her riding boots, grabbed her hat, and made herself a promise to e-mail Lara as soon as she got back from helping Comet look for Destiny.

Comet saw her coming toward the paddock and gave a whinny of welcome. The morning sun made his dapple-gray coat look like polished metal.

"Hi, Comet! We've got the whole morning to search for Destiny. Are you ready?" she sang out.

Comet tossed his head with eagerness, his deep-violet eyes flashing. "Yes, Marcie, but I need to do one thing first."

Marcie felt a warm prickling sensation flowing down to her fingertips as bright violet sparks bloomed in Comet's dapple-gray coat. There was a crackling sound and a flash of rainbow light, which quickly faded to reveal Comet standing there fully tacked-up.

"Wow! That's incredible," Marcie exclaimed at Comet's cleverness. He was full of surprises.

Comet pawed the ground. "Climb onto my back, Marcie."

Marcie checked that all the straps were tightened and then mounted. As the magic pony broke into a trot down to the far end of the paddock, Marcie moved in time to his strides. They reached the barred gate that led straight into Willow Lane, and Marcie opened it and closed it behind them.

A few feet down the quiet winding lane, she turned Comet onto a track that led along the edge of a field and then to open farmland. Marcie and Lara had often ridden Tramp here. She knew all the best bridleways through the woods and which farmers allowed riders to cross their land.

"Let's go, Comet!" Marcie cried, nudging him on.

Comet snorted eagerly, pulling at his bit, and sprang forward into a gallop.

Marcie crouched low on his back, her hair blowing in the warm breeze. Excitement raced through her. Comet was thrilling to ride, so smooth and exciting, and his warm magic seemed to spread around her, so that however fast they went, she felt perfectly safe.

Comet almost flew along, his hooves barely brushing the grass. His head turned

left and right as his sharp eyes searched
for any sign that Destiny had come this
way.

"Hold tight!" he told Marcie as he
surged up a slope that led to the crest of
a hill. At the top he paused, his mane
and tail stirring in the breeze, and then
plunged down the other side toward some
woods.

Marcie caught her breath, almost
laughing aloud with joy. Happiness
filled her. She loved nothing better in
the whole world than riding on a bright
sunny day.

Comet checked his stride and slowed
as they entered the shade of the trees.

Bright green ferns bordered the bridle
path on both sides and grew thickly
among the trees. They were so tall that

a dog or a very small pony could have
hidden beneath them. Marcie peered
into the undergrowth as they pressed on,
keeping a lookout, but there was no sign
of Destiny.

After a thorough search, they emerged
from the woods.

"I do not think she came this way,"
Comet said, scanning the shallow ridge
ahead of them, which was dotted with
grazing sheep.

Marcie spotted two small ponies
tethered in a field to one side. "Look!
Maybe Destiny is disguised as one of
those!" she cried.

Comet nickered with renewed
interest as he cantered over to investigate.
But neither of the shaggy little ponies was
Destiny. He trotted away sadly.

"I only hope that Destiny has found
a safe hiding place," Comet whinnied.
"The dark horses are always watching and
waiting to steal our magic."

"We'll find her. I know we will. There
are lots more places to search around here.
I'll show you." Marcie patted his neck and
then clicked her tongue encouragingly.

They rode on, taking a circular
route that eventually brought them back
through the woods.

"I think we'd better head home now,"
Marcie decided reluctantly. "Mom and
Dad will be back soon."

Comet nodded.

They retraced their steps, but skirted
the bottom of the hill. The track came
out farther down Willow Lane. Facing
them, Marcie could see the stone
pillars that marked the large gateway of
Blackberry Farm, which had been empty
for ages.

She noticed that there were cars
on the farmhouse drive and a woman
was putting curtains up at an upstairs
window. The stable block had been
freshly painted.

On impulse, she reined in Comet
and they stopped beside one of the stone
pillars, out of sight of the main house.

"It looks like new people have moved in," she commented. "I wonder what they're like."

Just then, a large muscular brown horse burst out of an open stable door. Tossing its head, it laid back its ears and raced toward them.

Chapter
FIVE

"Quick, Comet! We have to stop that
horse from getting out!" Marcie cried.
"The busy main road runs along the
bottom of Willow Lane!"

Comet stepped forward and stood
sideways to block the gateway.

The brown horse snorted as it slowed
to a halt a few feet away. Rolling its eyes,
it reared up onto its back legs.

"Watch out! It's going to kick!" Marcie warned, steeling herself for a painful blow as the horse's flailing hooves came within inches of hitting her leg. Though she was more scared that Comet would be hurt.

Pushing down on the stirrups, she stood up and waved her arms at the frightened horse, hoping it would turn aside and not try to bite or kick them.

Comet stood his ground. He turned
his head to look at the brown horse, and
Marcie felt another tingling sensation
flow down her fingers as violet sparks
glowed in Comet's dapple-gray coat. A
shimmering mist briefly surrounded the
horse and then gradually faded along with
every last violet spark.

The brown horse stood there, calm
now. Its dark eyes were soft and kind.
Comet gave a friendly blow and reached
out to touch noses gently
with it.

"Good job, Comet!" Marcie
dismounted and moved slowly toward
the loose horse. Luckily it wore a head
collar, so she reached up and grasped
hold. "Don't be scared. It's okay, I
won't hurt you," she said reassuringly.

To her relief, it didn't throw up its head or try to back away.

"You were very brave to try to stop that horse," Comet said to Marcie.

"I didn't really think about it. I couldn't bear the idea of you being hurt. Anyway, you were brave, too," she said, looking at Comet adoringly. "I think we saved each other!"

"Oh, thank goodness. You've caught her!"

A boy, who looked about twelve years old, was running up to Marcie and Comet. He had fair hair that flopped forward onto his forehead and an open, friendly face.

A younger girl came pounding after him. The girl caught up to the boy and stood there, breathing hard.

"What's happening? Is Drift all right?" she demanded, frowning.

The boy looked at her. "She's fine. Don't panic, Sally. Luckily, this girl caught her before she hurt herself." He took a lead rope out of his jeans pocket and clipped it on to the brown horse's head collar.

"And we're fine, too, thanks," Marcie

said drily. It had been pretty scary to have Drift run straight at her and Comet.

"Oh yeah. Sorry about that. Drift's a total sweetie, except when she's having one of her off days!" he said to Marcie with a narrow grin.

"Like today?" Marcie guessed, smiling. "I'm Marcie Locket. I live just up the road."

"Hi, Marcie. I'm Ian Bale, and this girl, who looks like she's just sucked a lemon, is my sister, Sally."

"Very funny. Not!" Sally shot back at him.

She also had fair hair, held back from her face by a brown velvet headband, and there was a sprinkle of freckles on her cheeks. She looked about nine years old and would have been very pretty if she hadn't been scowling fiercely.

"You total idiot, Ian. You should have kept your eye on Drift," Sally scolded her brother. "You know what she can be like. Here, I'll take her."

"Me? *You* left the stable door open!" Ian said.

"I did not!" Sally's cheeks flamed.

"Yes, you di—Oh, forget it," Ian said, shrugging. He obviously couldn't be bothered to get into an argument in front of Marcie and Comet. Sighing, he handed Sally the leading rope. "Suit yourself."

His sister flashed him a triumphant grin and then clicked her tongue at Drift. Turning on her heel, she led the horse back toward the stables.

"Oh, by the way, thanks," Sally murmured, not bothering to look back at Marcie.

"No problem," Marcie called after her.

Ian flashed Marcie a wry grin. "Don't mind Sally. She's a drama queen, but she never stays grumpy for long." He ran an appreciative eye over Comet. "He's a Connemara, isn't he? They're good all-rounders, aren't they? We used to have one. What's he called?"

"Comet," Marcie told him.

"Hello, boy." Ian put up his hand so Comet could nuzzle it. "How long have

you had him?" he asked Marcie.

"Not very long. Actually he's . . . um
. . . on loan," Marcie said vaguely, hoping
to avoid awkward questions. "I didn't know
that anyone had moved into Blackberry
Farm. How long have you been here?" she
asked, quickly changing the subject.

"Just a couple of weeks," Ian told her.
"I really like it here. It seems like there'll
be lots of good places to ride."

"There are," Marcie agreed. "I could
show you and Sally some, if you like. Do
you have any other horses or ponies besides
Drift?"

"Yeah, we've got Rufus and Fiddler, too.
Would you like to come and meet them?"

"I'd love to—" Marcie began, but then
she remembered that she was supposed to be
hurrying home before her parents returned

from shopping. "I can't now, though. I have to get back home."

"No problem," Ian said easily. "Why don't you come over tomorrow? Sally and I plan to go riding—if she's in a better mood, that is. You and Comet could come, too, and you can show us around."

"Sounds great," Marcie said, beaming. It would give her and Comet another chance to search for Destiny.

They arranged a time to meet up and then Marcie remounted Comet. "Bye!" She waved to Ian before they rode up the lane.

"Ian was really nice, wasn't he?" Marcie said, once they were out of earshot.

Comet nodded. "I like him, too."

"I'm not so sure about Sally, though," Marcie commented. "She seemed a bit grumpy. I hope Ian's right when he says

she's usually okay. I'm looking forward to
going riding with them tomorrow."

Comet's deep-violet eyes glowed under
his long eyelashes. Marcie knew he was
hoping he'd find Destiny.

Back home, she turned Comet out into
the paddock. There was a small fountain
of violet sparkles as the tack disappeared.
Comet shook himself and then walked
over to the trough for a long drink.

Marcie smiled at him. "I'll come
out to see you later and bring you some
carrots," she promised.

Inside the house, she quickly checked
that her mom and dad weren't home and
then dumped her riding boots and hat in
the utility room. After grabbing a cold
drink, she went and sat at the family

computer to write to Lara. She wished she
could tell her all about the magical time
she had been having with Comet!

Marcie was halfway through her
e-mail when she heard a car door slam.
She looked out the window to see her
dad coming up the drive carrying bags of
groceries.

The front door opened, and then he
stuck his head around the sitting-room
door. "Are you still on that computer,
young lady? You must have an awful lot to
tell Lara!" he teased.

Marcie beamed at him. "I do!" *If only
you knew*, she thought. "Guess what? I
just met the two kids who moved into
Blackberry Farm: Sally and Ian Bale,"
she told him, her enthusiasm running
away with her. "And they've got a horse

and two ponies! I've got some new horsey friends, and they live just down the road!"

Mr. Locket looked puzzled. "Really? Well, that is a bit of good luck, especially now that Lara isn't here. But how come you met Ian and Sally? I thought you said you'd be staying in the house. You know the rules about always letting us know where you are when you go out," he said sternly.

Marcie realized her mistake. She thought fast. She could hardly tell her dad that she'd been perfectly safe because she was with Comet. "Um . . . no, I didn't exactly go anywhere," she lied. "They . . . uh . . . came past on their ponies and I just went outside onto the driveway to talk to them. In fact, they asked me to go riding with them tomorrow!"

Chapter SIX

Marcie woke early the following
morning to find sunshine streaming
through a gap in the curtains.

"Yay! I'm going riding again on
Comet!" she said to herself as she leaped
out of bed and quickly dressed in jeans
and a T-shirt.

Her dad was already downstairs when
Marcie appeared. The delicious smell of

frying bacon met her as she opened the kitchen door.

"Dad! You're up early," Marcie said, surprised. He usually liked to sleep in on Sundays.

He smiled, looking a bit weary. "I didn't sleep very well with so much on my mind. So I thought I'd make breakfast. Bacon-and-egg sandwiches are on the menu, if you're interested."

"You bet! Can I cut the bread?" Marcie asked helpfully.

"Thanks, sweetie. You must be looking forward to meeting up with your new friends. It's nice of them to invite you riding with them," he commented.

"Yes, it is." Marcie flipped her hair over her shoulder as she wielded the bread knife. The slices were a bit uneven, but

her dad didn't seem to notice.

As soon as she'd finished breakfast, Marcie put on her riding gear and then said good-bye to her parents. "See you later! I'll take the shortcut across the paddock."

She felt a thrill of excitement when she saw Comet standing with his head over the fence waiting for her. As she approached him, Comet curled his dark gray lips and greeted her with a neigh of welcome. He was already tacked-up and eager to go.

Marcie swung herself into the saddle and leaned over to pat his silky neck as they set off.

Ian and Sally were waiting for them in the stable yard. Ian was on a handsome chestnut pony with two white socks. Marcie guessed that this was Rufus. He waved as she and Comet rode through the front gates.

"Hi, Marcie!" Sally waved, too. She was just mounting a pretty palomino.

"What a lovely pony!" Marcie said, pleased to see that Sally seemed in a better mood today.

Sally smiled, her blue eyes sparkling. "Thanks. Fiddler's really sweet."

"We usually take turns exercising the ponies," Ian told her, controlling Rufus as the chestnut pony sidestepped.

"Poor old Drift doesn't look too happy at being left behind."

Marcie glanced to where the big brown horse was standing with her head over the paddock fence, watching them with mournful dark eyes. As Ian and Sally rode out onto Willow Lane in single file, Marcie gave Drift one last sympathetic look before following behind the others.

"I thought we could ride up to the old water tower on the hill. The view is great from up there," Marcie said. It was also in the opposite direction of where she and Comet had already searched, which meant they would be able to explore a different area.

"I hope we'll find Destiny this time or some sign that she came this way," she whispered to him as they reached the main road and waited at the crossing.

"I hope so, too!" Comet replied.

Marcie froze, surprised that he had spoken aloud to her with Ian and Sally so close. But neither of them seemed to have noticed anything odd.

"Do not worry, Marcie," Comet told her, as if he knew what she was thinking. "Only you can hear me speaking.

Everyone else will just think I am
neighing or snorting."

"Cool!" Marcie whispered in reply,
relaxing.

Once safely across the main road,
Marcie took a side turn and led the way
down a wide, grassy track lined with
hedges. The hawthorn was still covered
with clusters of creamy flowers. Their
sweet, musty scent filled the air.

After a few miles the track opened
out onto a sweep of hillside covered with
sparse-looking grass. Marcie squeezed
Comet into a gallop and Ian and Sally did
the same. Rabbits dived for cover as the
ponies sped past.

Ahead of them the ground rose
steeply to where an old stone building
topped the hill.

"Race you to the top!" Sally cried, crouching low on Fiddler.

"You're on! Whoo-hoo!" Ian yelled, urging Rufus forward.

Comet couldn't resist. He shot after the ponies in a lightning burst of speed. In a thunder of hooves, he streaked past them, his dark gray tail flying out behind him like a silken banner.

"Yay! Eat our dust!" Marcie yelled over her shoulder.

Rufus and Fiddler stretched out and gave chase, but they couldn't match Comet's powerful stride. Marcie thought she noticed the shadow of a large horse spreading across the hillside as Comet raced past, but then it was gone, so she must have imagined it. They reached the top of the hill, twenty feet ahead of the others. She reined Comet in beside the water tower and they stood waiting for Ian and Sally.

"What kept you?" Marcie joked as they rode up.

Ian laughed. "I thought Rufus was fast, but Comet can *really* move!" he said admiringly.

"That was fun!" Sally said, her face glowing.

They sat in a line looking out at the

view over the green rolling hills. In the distance they could see a gray smudge where the hills met the sky.

Marcie wondered where Destiny could be hiding in this wide-open space, broken only by isolated farms and the occasional cow shed or barn.

They continued on, riding more slowly and enjoying the fresh air and sunshine. In the fold of two hills, there was a fast-running stream and they stopped to let the ponies drink.

Marcie bent close to whisper to Comet. "I haven't seen any signs that Destiny's been this way. Have you?"

Comet shook his head, twitching one ear disappointedly. "Not yet."

An hour later, Ian announced that he

was hungry and suggested they go back to Blackberry Farm for lunch. And with rumbling tummies, everyone agreed.

Back at the farm, Ian and Sally untacked their ponies. Drift lifted her head and nickered a welcome from the paddock, seemingly very pleased not to be by herself any longer. As the ponies all seemed to be getting along well together, Ian suggested that Marcie turn out Comet with them.

Mrs. Bale made an enormous and hearty lunch, which they ate at a big wooden table in the farmhouse kitchen. Salad and baked potatoes with cheese, followed by homemade vanilla cupcakes with chocolate frosting, all washed down with lemonade. After lunch, Sally took Marcie up to her bedroom and

excitedly showed her all the ribbons and
trophies she'd won on Fiddler. Marcie
found herself having the best time she'd
had since Lara had lived in her town.
She would have liked to stay longer, but
thought she'd better check that Comet
was still happy at being left in the Bales'
paddock with the other ponies.

Sally walked out to the stable yard
with her. "I had a great time today," she
said, a smile lighting up her pretty face.

"Me too," Marcie said. "Thanks for showing me your trophies and stuff."

"Of course. I just got a great new book about braiding manes and tails. You can borrow it sometime, if you'd like."

"That sounds cool. Thanks," Marcie said warmly, pleased that she and Sally were now getting along so well. Maybe she'd ask her to come over soon and they could watch her favorite movie, *Black Beauty*.

Ian was in the tack room, hanging up clean bridles and folding horse blankets. "I'll do this all by myself, then, huh?" he teased, rolling his eyes at his sister.

"Yeah! Why don't you?" Sally gave him a playful shove, but began helping him.

Marcie grinned. Those two were a double act! Shaking her head slowly, she walked the few feet to the paddock.

"Are you ready to go home now?" she whispered to Comet.

"Yes. I thought I might go out searching for Destiny again," Comet told her. "But I do not think you should come with me, as I sensed the dark horses' presence earlier."

Marcie felt a prickle of concern. So she hadn't been imagining things—that dark shadow was real. Would Comet's magic be strong enough to protect him from his enemies when he was so far from home?

Her mind was filled by this worrying thought as she led him out and let the paddock gate shut itself behind her with a soft click.

Chapter SEVEN

As it was getting dark, Marcie slipped into the garden to check that Comet had returned after his latest search.

To her relief he was there, his gray coat gleaming softly in the moonlight. Her heart swelled with happiness and pride as she looked at him. She didn't think she'd ever get over the incredible feeling of being friends with a magic pony.

"Greetings, Marcie," Comet snorted softly.

"I was worried about you," she admitted. "What would happen if the dark horses found you while you were looking for Destiny?" she asked him.

"Before I came here I looked into the Stone of Power to see where Destiny was. Its magic still gives me some protection," he told her.

Reassured, Marcie gave him some pieces of carrot from her pocket. Comet crunched them up eagerly. She spent a few more minutes with him, saying good night, and then hurried back indoors before her parents noticed she was gone.

Mr. Locket had just finished using the computer.

Marcie asked if she could use it and e-mailed Lara to tell her about her ride with Ian and Sally. She didn't mention Comet, but said that she'd borrowed Drift to ride. She sent the message, and after a couple of minutes, Lara e-mailed back to say that she'd love to meet Ian, Sally, and their ponies when she came to visit. Marcie signed out and then logged off. She was feeling happier than she had for some time as she went upstairs to read for a while before going to bed. But she had only just opened her book, when she heard a loud knock on the front door.

She sat up, frowning. Who could it be this late?

Marcie came out of her bedroom as her dad answered the door.

Ian's panicky voice floated up to her. "Is Marcie there? All the ponies have escaped! Can she come and help us look for them?"

"Oh no!" Marcie ran down the stairs. "What happened? How did they get out?" Ian avoided her eyes.

"Um . . . it doesn't really matter. Sally's already out looking for them with Mom and Dad. I came to ask you to help because you know the area better than we do."

"I'll go grab a flashlight!" Marcie
turned to her mom and dad. "It's okay if I
go, isn't it?"

They nodded. "Of course you should
help, but you can't go out in the middle of
the night by yourself," her dad said.

"We'll come, too," her mom decided.

After grabbing coats, boots, and
flashlights, Marcie, Ian, and her mom and
dad set out. They walked around the road
and turned into the top of Willow Lane.
Sally and her mom came hurrying up to
them.

"Any sign of the ponies?" Ian asked his
sister.

In the dim light Sally's face looked
pale and drawn. She shook her head. "Dad
thinks they might have cut across the fields
opposite ours. He went to look." Her voice

broke into a sob. "Oh, I hope they did. I can't bear to think about them getting out onto the main road . . ."

Marcie went to put a comforting hand on Sally's arm.

But Sally twisted away distractedly. "Don't touch me!" she snapped.

Marcie tried not to feel hurt. Sally must have been so upset that she hardly knew what she was saying. Marcie didn't blame her. She knew she'd be crazy with worry if anything happened to Comet.

Comet! He would find the missing ponies in no time, but how could she get away from the others and go to ask him for his help?

"I'll . . . um . . . check on this side," Marcie decided on impulse. "Dad? Why don't you and Mom get the car and meet me down at the other field. The one with the gate that leads out to the main road."

"It makes sense to split up," her mom agreed. "And Marcie knows these fields like the back of her hand." She turned to Marcie. "Don't take any risks, sweetie. If you see any sign of the ponies, stand still and keep turning your flashlight on and off until someone comes to help you."

"I will," Marcie promised, already pointing the flashlight to illuminate her way as she walked over the cattle guard into the first field.

She crossed her fingers, hoping that none of the others would follow. Luckily, Ian went off with Sally and their mom, while Marcie's parents headed for their garage. Marcie was about to head back toward Comet's paddock, when her fingers began to tingle and Comet himself appeared beside her in a cloud of shimmering rainbow mist.

"Comet! What are you doing here? I was just about to come and look for you!"

"I heard all the voices and guessed what had happened. Hurry! Climb on my back, Marcie! Do not worry. I have used my magic to make you invisible too when you are riding me."

Marcie mounted. She twisted her hands into his dark gray mane and held on tight.

"I'm ready!"

Comet sped away, moving as fast as the wind. A protective bubble of rainbow sparkles surrounded Marcie, keeping her safe on top of Comet's back. One. Two.

Three. The fields rushed past in a
magical blur. There was no sign of the
ponies.

Down in the field, Comet raced
alongside the tall hedges toward the
gate. They had to find the ponies before
they reached it and were spooked by the
traffic in the road beyond. Comet sped
on, his flashing hooves eating up the
ground.

Suddenly, Marcie spotted three
shadowy fast-moving shapes in the
distance.

"Look, there's Drift, Rufus, and
Fiddler!" she gasped. "Thank goodness
they're all together."

"I see them, too," Comet neighed.

Leaping forward in another dizzying
burst of speed, he easily closed the

distance between them. Comet rode up alongside the terrified ponies. Marcie's fingers tingled again as he sent out an invisible spray of violet sparks that settled on them like soft rain.

The runaway ponies gradually slowed to a trot and then a walking pace. Finally they stopped, their sides heaving.

Marcie was still worried. Any one of the ponies could get scared by a sudden noise and bolt again. And the gate to the main road was horribly close.

"Do you think you could use your magic to make them follow you?" she asked urgently.

Comet nodded. "I have an idea. This way they will get to safety more quickly."

There was another violet flash of Comet's sparkly magic, and rainbow

shimmers whirled around them all. Marcie
felt the air whistle past her ears as they all
found themselves flying through the night
with the stars twinkling above them.
There was a slight jolt as Comet's hooves
touched down farther up the field. The
other ponies were safely beside him.

"Wow! You were amazing, Comet!"
Marcie said, dismounting.

"I am glad I could help."

She was reaching up to hug him, when

she felt him stiffen and lean down to stare
at the grass.

Marcie looked down, too. In front of
them both and stretching away up the hill
was a faint line of softly glowing violet
hoofprints.

"Destiny! She came this way!" Comet
whinnied excitedly.

Marcie felt a pang. Did that mean that
he was leaving, right now? "Are . . . are
you going after her?" she asked anxiously.

Comet shook his head. "No. The trail
is cold. But it proves Destiny was here,"
he said, his eyes glowing with fresh hope.
"When she is very close, I will be able to
hear her hoofbeats. And then I may have
to leave suddenly, without saying good-
bye."

Marcie bit her lip as she realized

she had secretly been hoping that he
might stay forever. "Couldn't you and
Destiny live here with me and share your
paddock?" she asked hopefully.

"No, Marcie, that is not possible. We
must return to our family on Rainbow
Mist Island," Comet explained gently.

Marcie swallowed hard, feeling
tears well up. "I guess I knew that," she
admitted. She forced herself to smile as

she decided not to think about Comet leaving and to enjoy every moment with him.

Just then a car swung off the main road and pulled into the gateway. Its headlights streamed into the field onto Marcie, Comet, and the ponies. Marcie felt herself tense and then relax again as she remembered that Comet was invisible to everyone except her.

"I am not needed now. I will see you tomorrow, Marcie." Comet disappeared in a final shower of violet sparkles that glistened as they fell around Marcie's feet.

"Marcie! You found them!" Her mom and dad had opened the gate and were walking toward her. Moments later, Ian, Sally, and Mr. and Mrs. Bale appeared at the top of the field, their flashlights

wobbling as they came running toward
the Lockets from the opposite direction.

"There they are! It's our ponies!" Sally
cried, dashing forward.

Fiddler nickered softly as she saw her.
Sally flung her arms around the palomino's
neck and burst into tears of relief.

"It's okay, Sally. Fiddler isn't injured.
They're all fine," Marcie said reassuringly.

She wished she could have told Sally
about how amazing Comet had been,
but of course, she never would.

Sally turned to Marcie, her face
twisted in anger. "No thanks to you! It
was your fault in the first place! You left
the paddock gate unlatched. That's why
the ponies escaped!"

Chapter
EIGHT

Marcie blinked at Sally in shock and dismay.

"I . . . I didn't. I closed the paddock gate after I let Com—" she began and broke off in confusion, as she remembered that she couldn't mention the magic pony in front of her parents. They had no idea that he even existed.

Sally's lip curled. "You obviously

didn't bother to check if it was closed properly. Don't try and get out of this. You could at least say sorry!"

"I would apologize, but I honestly don't think I left the gate open," Marcie said reasonably.

But Sally was too wound up to listen. "I don't believe you! Stay away from me. I don't want to talk to you!" she shouted. She whirled around and stomped away.

Marcie watched her go, speechless. "Ian. You believe me, don't you?" She turned to him, hoping that he would listen to her.

But he shrugged and looked very embarrassed. "I . . . I don't know, Marcie. Leave it for now. You can't get through to Sally when she's like this," he said. He turned to his dad. "Let's get the ponies home."

Mr. Bale nodded. He thanked Marcie's mom and dad for helping to search for the ponies.

Mrs. Bale turned to Marcie. "Whatever did happen, no harm's done. Don't worry about it now. Let's all go home," she suggested.

"Everything will seem clearer after a good night's sleep," Mrs. Locket agreed. "Come on, Marcie. We'll all drive back."

Marcie's heart was heavy as she trudged through the gate and went toward the car with her parents. "I don't get it. Why is everyone blaming me?" she gulped, close to tears.

"They're tired and upset," her dad soothed. "I suggest you go see Ian and Sally when they've had a chance to calm down."

"It won't do any good. I know what Sally's like. She hates me now," Marcie said miserably.

Their promising new friendship looked like it was over before it had even begun.

Over the next few days, Marcie racked her brain, trying to remember whether she had left the Bales' paddock gate open.

She was talking to Comet one morning before she left for school. "I remember that I was worried about you meeting those horrible dark horses when I let you out of the Bales' paddock. Maybe I wasn't concentrating and I left the gate off the latch. If I'm honest, I'm not even sure anymore."

Comet's deep-violet eyes softened. "Even if you did, it was not done deliberately."

"Try telling Sally that," Marcie said sadly. "I've gone over twice after school and called, but she won't even talk to me. She's my best friend here now that Lara's moved away. No one at school loves ponies as much as we do! Even Ian's only just about speaking to me, and I'm sure he's just being polite. I know he secretly blames me for letting the ponies escape. I feel awful!"

Comet leaned toward her and huffed out a soft warm breath. "You are a kind person and good friend."

Marcie felt herself calming down as she stroked his velvety dark-gray muzzle.

"Thanks for believing in me. You're the best friend anyone could have," she said fondly.

Comet fell silent and his ears swiveled thoughtfully.

"What?" Marcie asked.

"Do you remember the day we met Ian and Sally at the farm gateway?"

Marcie nodded. How could she forget? "You stopped Drift from hurting us and galloping out into Willow Lane, didn't you? Sally and Ian were arguing about who'd left the stable door open."

"That is right." Comet's mane stirred in the breeze. "Did they not also say that Drift could be difficult?"

"Yes," Marcie agreed, trying to remember exactly what the Bales had said about the big brown horse. "I got the impression that she likes escaping and running off."

"That is what I thought." Comet

snorted in satisfaction, his eyes twinkling mysteriously.

Marcie frowned, still puzzled. What was Comet getting at?

"I think you should go and see Ian and Sally again," Comet decided, swishing his tail.

"Really? I'm not sure it would do any good," Marcie said doubtfully, but she trusted Comet's judgment. "I will, if you think I should."

Comet nodded. "I do, Marcie. Friendship is important. Is it not worth fighting for?"

"I guess it is," Marcie agreed. "I'll give it one more try, and this time I'm not leaving until Sally agrees to talk to me. We'll go over to Blackberry Farm as soon as I get home after school. Okay?"

Comet nodded, his eyes shining with wisdom.

Marcie was so nervous about their plan to go and see Sally and Ian that she could hardly concentrate in class.

Somehow she managed to get through her schoolwork. Luckily, they were working on their projects. Marcie's was about heavy horses and their lives, so she found herself enjoying writing a page about shire horses. It was a surprise when the bell rang for the end of class and she could rush out to meet her mom.

"You seem a bit more cheerful," Mrs. Locket said as she parked the car in their driveway. "Did you make up with Ian and Sally?"

"Not yet. But I'm working on it!"

She changed out of her school clothes and was about to go out to Comet when the house phone rang.

Her mom picked it up.

Marcie heard her say, "When did this happen?" *It's your dad*, Mrs. Locket mouthed at her silently.

Marcie crossed her fingers and toes for good luck as she waited for her mom to put the phone down. *Please, please let it be good news*, she prayed. Mrs. Locket took a deep breath and stood with her hand on her chest. Marcie almost exploded with impatience.

"Mo-om! What's going on?"

"I can hardly believe it myself," her mom said, blinking dazedly. "Your dad's just been offered a new job, much better than his last one. He starts next week.

It pays a lot more than he's been getting. So I think you can start looking at ponies for sale!"

"Really? Yay! That's amazing! Good for Dad!" Marcie squealed. She grabbed her mom and they did a triumphant little dance up and down the hall.

She was going to get her pony, and
Comet would have a new friend to share
the paddock with! She couldn't wait to
e-mail Lara and tell her the fabulous news,
not mentioning Comet, of course. But
first, she was going to Blackberry Farm.

"I'm going to make Sally see what
she's missing by not being my friend," she
told her mom determinedly.

"Good for you, sweetie. That's the
way. It might be tough to get her to talk
to you, though. Do you want me to come
with you?"

"No. I have to do this on my own,"
Marcie said firmly, already halfway out of
the door. "I won't be long."

At the paddock, she told Comet the
good news about her dad's new job.

His intelligent eyes shone. "That is

wonderful, Marcie. What sort of pony would you like?"

"A Connemara, of course! What else?" Marcie said immediately. "Everything's getting better now. It would be just perfect if Ian and Sally wanted to be friends with me again."

Comet didn't reply. He tossed his head, and in a flash and a cloud of violet sparkles he was fully tacked-up. "Climb on my back, Marcie!" he neighed.

As they rode out onto Willow Lane, Marcie's bright self-confidence wavered. What if Sally still wasn't prepared to listen to her?

They had reached the curve in the road, just before Blackberry Farm, when Marcie heard a sound she had been longing for and dreading at the same time.

The hollow sound of hooves galloping overhead.

"Destiny!" Comet veered off into the nearby field, following the magical hoofbeats, which sounded louder and closer. Panting with excitement, he halted briefly beside a hedge.

"You must get down now, Marcie," he told her gently. Marcie dismounted. She knew that this time he was leaving. Her heart ached with sadness, but she knew she would have to be very strong.

There was a violet flash, and a twinkling rainbow mist floated down around Comet. He stood there in his true form, a dapple-gray pony no longer, but a magnificent magic pony with a noble head, cream coat, and spreading golden wings. His golden mane and tail flowed down in shimmering silken strands.

"Comet!" Marcie gasped. She had almost forgotten how beautiful he was.

"I hope you catch Destiny. Good luck! I'll never forget you!" she said, her voice breaking.

Comet's deep-violet eyes clouded
over for a moment with sadness.
"Farewell, young friend. Ride well and
true," he said in a deep musical voice.

There was a final violet flash of light
and a silent burst of rainbow sparkles
that showered down around Marcie in
crystal droplets and tinkled as they hit
the grass.

Comet spread his wings and soared
upward. He faded and was gone.

Marcie gulped back tears, hardly
able to believe that this had happened so
fast. Something glittered on the grass.
It was a single shimmering gold wing-
feather. Reaching down, she picked it
up. It tingled against her palm as it faded
to a cream color. She slipped it into her
pocket, knowing that she would treasure

it always as a reminder of the wonderful adventure she had shared with the magic pony.

As Marcie stepped back out onto Willow Lane, Sally waved at her from the farm gate.

"Marcie! Come here," she cried. "I have something to show you!"

Quickly wiping her eyes, Marcie followed. Sally didn't seem to be quite as angry with her right now. Marcie was puzzled.

Ian was standing by the stable door, just out of sight of Fiddler, Rufus, and Drift in the nearby paddock. He gestured to Marcie to be quiet. "Watch this," he whispered, pointing at Drift.

The brown horse pricked her ears. She walked up to the gate. Leaning her weight against the catch, Drift used her teeth to spring it, so that the gate swung slowly open. Ian quickly rushed forward, closed it again, and slipped a loop of rope over it, before she could escape.

Marcie blinked in astonishment. "So that's how all the ponies got out!"

"Yes. It was Drift. She can open doors and gates. I'm so sorry that I blamed you. I've been so mean, haven't I?" Sally said.

Marcie realized that Comet had worked all this out. This was his final gift to her before he had to leave forever.

"Who cares?" Grinning widely, she gave Sally a big hug. "I'm just glad we can be friends again!"

You were right, Comet! Marcie said
silently. *Friendship is worth fighting for.*
Wherever he was, she knew that his
deep-violet eyes would be shining with
approval.

Magic Ponies

A Twinkle of Hooves

SUE BENTLEY

Prologue

Comet folded his gold-feathered wings as his hooves touched down on the grass of his magical island home. The magic pony felt excited. Surely his twin sister was here, safely among the Lightning Herd once again.

"I can't wait to see Destiny! She has been lost for so long," Comet cried, his violet eyes flashing.

It was a hot day and he was thirsty. Trotting toward a crystal stream, he drank deeply. Sunlight, filtering through a nearby birch tree, gleamed on his cream coat and flowing golden mane and tail.

Lifting his head, he peered through the woods on the far side of the stream. Beyond them the magic pony could see gently rolling hills and the tops of the snowcapped mountains, wreathed in the softly shimmering, multicolored clouds that gave Rainbow Mist Island its name.

Suddenly, the trees swayed as a shadowy shape moved through them. Comet twitched his ears forward eagerly.

"Destiny?"

There was no answer. Puzzled, he took a step and then stopped in alarm. Perhaps it was one of the dark horses, waiting in ambush! They were always plotting to steal the Lightning Horses' magic.

Tremors flickered over Comet's silky coat, and he flexed his magnificent golden wings, ready to soar away to safety.

An older cream-and-gold horse with a wise expression and glowing dark eyes stepped out of the trees and splashed across the stream toward him.

"Blaze!" Comet cried in relief. He bent his head in greeting before the leader of the Lightning Herd.

Blaze's eyes softened with affection. "I am glad to see you again, my young friend. Have you brought Destiny back with you?" he asked in a deep, velvety neigh.

"No. I was hoping that she had returned by herself," Comet told him sadly. "But I see now that I was mistaken."

Blaze looked at him gravely. "I do not think Destiny will ever come back, unless you find her and explain that the stone has been found."

The Stone of Power protected the Lightning Herd from the evil dark horses. Destiny had accidentally lost it during a game of cloud-racing with Comet. Comet found the stone, but Destiny had already fled in panic, thinking she was in a lot of trouble.

"I must look for her again," Comet decided. "She is in danger from the dark horses!"

Blaze pawed at the ground with one shining hoof. There was a flash of rainbow light and a beautiful fiery opal appeared.

"Come closer, Comet. Look into the

stone," Blaze neighed.

The magic pony moved nearer to the Stone of Power. He felt warm tingles move over his body as the stone grew larger and rays of dazzling rainbow light spread out from it. Comet gasped as he saw an image of Destiny form, galloping along a track beside redbrick houses, in a world far away.

There was a bright flash of violet light, and suddenly a rainbow mist surrounded Comet. The young cream pony with his flowing golden mane and powerful gleaming gold wings disappeared. In his place stood a small black-and-white pony with a broad white stripe down his black face.

"Use this disguise to protect yourself as you go into the other world. Go now, my young friend," urged Blaze.

"I will find Destiny and bring her back!" Comet vowed.

The pony's black-and-white coat bloomed with violet sparks, and a rainbow mist surrounded him. Comet neighed softly as he felt the power building inside him. The shimmering mist swirled faster and faster as it drew him in . . .

Chapter ONE

"Bye, Alice! I hope you and Fleur will be really happy!" Steph Danes called, her voice catching. She waved to the six-year-old girl who sat in the front seat of the car parked outside her house.

"Thank you. We will!" The little girl waved back, her small face shining with happiness.

Steph's eyes pricked with tears as the

car and the horse trailer it was towing
moved slowly away up Porlock Close. She
watched until they were out of sight, and
then her face crumpled as she turned to
her mom.

Mrs. Danes gave her daughter a hug
and stroked her short fair hair. "Good job,

honey. I know it was hard for you to let Fleur go. But we don't have the room to keep a pony you won't be riding anymore."

"I know." Steph sighed, wiping her eyes. "And Fleur's going to a good home. Alice really seemed to love her, didn't she?"

Her mom nodded, smiling fondly. "All little girls love their very own first pony the best. You were Alice's age when we got Fleur. It's too bad that you've outgrown her, but it happens to everyone eventually."

Steph nodded. She knew her mom was right, but she was going to miss Fleur, her little chestnut Dartmoor pony, like crazy. They'd had so much fun together in the last three years. Steph was going to feel very lonely not seeing her every day.

Steph and her mom walked back into

the house together. It was hot in the kitchen with the bright sun pouring in through the open back door. Steph got them cold drinks from the fridge.

She stared into space as she drank, feeling sad. Saturdays were usually for riding, and then grooming Fleur until her chestnut coat gleamed.

"Do you want to clear out the stable?" Mrs. Danes asked. "You could practice what you learned at that workshop on stable management over spring break."

Steph had really enjoyed the workshop. She wanted to work with horses when she grew up. "I guess I could do that now," she answered, deciding to get the upsetting task of removing all traces of Fleur over and done with.

Steph went outside to the old garage

at the side of the house. Her dad had converted it into a stable when they'd had the driveway extended and a bigger garage built. As she forked up soiled bedding and began to wheel it away, she felt an overwhelming wave of sadness. Fleur wasn't even here to appreciate what she was doing.

What was Steph going to do now without her very own little pony to look after and love? She sighed heavily before giving the stable floor one last mopping, but as she did a car drove up the cul-de-sac and pulled into the driveway.

Her dad got out and walked around to her. "Hello, sweetie. Keeping busy?" he asked.

Steph nodded. "I'm almost done. It's horrible, though, without Fleur."

"It must be," Mr. Danes agreed sympathetically. "We'll all miss her." He gave her a hug. "I knew you'd need cheering up, so I popped into the new riding stables in the village. Judy Marshall, the owner, says they aren't too busy today. You can go right over and have your pick of the ponies to ride."

Steph stared at him in surprise. How could he even think that she'd want to ride a pony she didn't know? It was far too soon. She'd feel disloyal to Fleur.

"I don't really feel like it right now. Maybe some other time," she murmured.

"I don't like to think of you sitting around brooding," her dad said kindly. "Why don't you give the new stables a try? Riding's what you love doing the most, after all, isn't it?" he asked gently.

"Well, yes—usually," Steph admitted. She still wasn't sure that this was a good idea, but her dad had gone out of his way to get her a ride and she didn't want to hurt his feelings. "I guess I could go over there and take a look."

"That's the spirit! Come on, grab your riding gear. I'll have a quick word with your mom. See you in the car."

Despite herself, Steph felt a bit brighter because of his enthusiasm. Maybe getting to know some new ponies would be fun and help her miss Fleur less—at least for a little while. "Okay." She sighed. "Thanks, Dad."

She went into the house, put on her boots, and came back out holding her riding hat by the chin strap.

"All set!" Mr. Danes started the engine.

It was only a few minutes' drive to
Marshall's Stables. Mr. Danes and Steph
went toward the office just as Judy
Marshall was coming out. She was a slim
woman with dark hair, a round face, and
friendly blue eyes.

"Hi! You must be Steph. Nice to meet
you," she said, smiling.

"Nice to meet you, too, Mrs. Marshall,"

Steph said, making an effort to be polite.
She still wasn't sure that she wanted to do
this.

"Call me Judy. Everyone does. Come
and meet the ponies." She turned to Mr.
Danes. "Steph will be fine now. We'll
look after her."

"See you later then, sweetie. Have a
good time."

"Bye, Dad." Steph watched him walk
away and then followed Judy toward the
main stable block.

The smart redbrick buildings were
around two sides of a square. Two smallish
ponies were tied up outside the tack room.
A boy and a girl in riding gear stood
waiting to mount.

"Judy? Someone's on the phone for
you!" a voice called.

"Coming!" Judy answered. She
turned to Steph. "Sorry, but I need to
take this call. Why don't you have a look
around? Just check with a staff member
before you take a pony out, okay?"

Steph nodded, smiling awkwardly.
"Thanks, Judy."

She walked toward the loose boxes.
The ponies turned to look at her,
twitching their ears curiously. Steph
went along the row, stroking and
patting each one in turn. Their names
were on the doors: Jiggy, Binky, Misty,
Lady, and Rags. They were all nice, but
none of them were Fleur. She fondly
remembered the little chestnut pony's
silky mane.

At the end of the row, there was an
empty box. As Steph reached it there was

a bright flash, and sparkling rainbow mist filled the walls of the box. Rainbow drops settled on her skin, glittering in the afternoon light.

"Oh!" Steph blinked, trying to see through the strange mist.

As it slowly cleared, she saw that there was in fact a pony in there after all. It was a handsome black-and-white piebald with a broad white stripe down its nose and

large deep-violet eyes. How could she have missed it before? But Steph couldn't deny he was there now, and as the pony looked at her inquisitively, Steph felt her heart melt just a little.

"Hello, you!" she crooned gently. She'd never seen a pony with eyes that color. Maybe she could ride him. *But just so I can tell Dad that I did*, Steph thought quickly.

Opening the door, she went inside and lifted her hand to stroke the pony's satiny cheek. It turned to look at her.

"Can you help me, please?" it asked in a velvety neigh.

Chapter TWO

Steph dropped her hand and looked
at the black-and-white pony in complete
shock. She must be imagining things.
Whoever heard of a pony that could talk?

"I wonder what your name is," she
murmured. It wasn't written on the door
like all the others.

The pony's eyes glowed brightly as it
lifted its head. "I am called Comet. And

I have arrived from Rainbow Mist Island.
What is your name?"

Steph did a double take. She hadn't
imagined it. This pony actually was speaking
to her! His large intelligent eyes gazed at
her and he blew out a quizzical breath, as if
waiting for her reply.

"I–I'm Steph. Steph Danes. I'm . . . um,
here for a riding lesson," she found herself
stammering.

"I am honored to meet you, Steph,"
Comet said, bowing his head.

"M–Me too," Steph said, still not quite
believing this was happening. Talking ponies
belonged in fairy tales or fantasy movies.
"Where did you say you came from?"

"Rainbow Mist Island. It is a place far
away, where I live with the other Lightning
Horses."

Steph's curiosity was starting to get the better of her shock. "So . . . how come you're here in Marshall's Stables?"

Comet glanced around at his surroundings. His long lashes blinked as he looked over the brick walls and clean straw on the floor. "Is that where I am? I have come to find Destiny, my twin sister."

"Is she here at the riding stable, too?" Steph asked.

"No, I do not think she is here in these stables, but she is hiding somewhere nearby in your world," Comet explained with a flick of his black tail. "She fled after she accidentally lost the Stone of Power, which protects our Lightning Herd. My twin sister and I were cloud-racing in the night sky when she dropped the stone. She thought it was lost forever. I found it, but Destiny does not know this. She is afraid to come home because she thinks she is in a lot of trouble."

Steph nodded slowly. "You say you and Destiny were *cloud-racing*? But how . . . ?"

"I will show you," Comet said, backing away.

Steph felt a strange warm tingling

sensation flow down to her fingertips
as violet-colored sparkles glittered in
Comet's black-and-white coat and streaks
of rainbow mist wove around him. The
handsome piebald pony disappeared, and
in its place, almost filling the loose box,
stood an elegant young cream-colored
pony with a flowing gold mane and tail.

Springing from its shoulders were folded wings, covered with shimmering golden feathers.

"Oh!" Steph caught her breath. She had never seen anything so wonderful in her entire life.

"Comet?" she gasped.

"Yes, Steph. It is still me. Do not be afraid." Comet gave a deep, musical whinny.

Before Steph could get used to the sight of the beautiful winged pony, there was a final swirl of sparkling mist and Comet reappeared as the handsome black-and-white piebald pony.

"That's a great disguise! Can Destiny make herself look like an ordinary pony, too?" Steph asked.

Comet nodded slowly. "Yes, but that

will not save her if the dark horses who want to steal our magic discover her," he explained. "I must find Destiny and take her back to Rainbow Mist Island before they do. Will you help me?"

Steph thought about it. Her heart was still aching for Fleur, so she knew how it felt to miss someone she loved. "Okay, I'll search for Destiny with you," she decided. To her surprise, she was actually starting to feel quite proud that this amazing magic pony had chosen to reveal himself to her. "Wait until I tell Mom and Dad about you. They won't believe it—"

"No. You cannot tell anyone about me or what I have told you!" Comet looked at her with serious eyes.

Steph felt disappointed. She was already keeping a secret about how much she

missed Fleur from her mom and dad;
she felt bad keeping another. But Comet
was right, this probably wasn't the sort of
thing that a grown-up would believe!

"You must promise me," Comet
insisted gently.

"Well . . . okay then. Cross my heart.
No one's going to hear about you from
me." Steph was prepared to agree if it
would help protect Comet and Destiny
until they returned together to Rainbow
Mist Island.

"Steph? Are you still here?" Judy
Marshall's voice rang out as she strode
across the stable yard, obviously having
finished her telephone conversation.

Inside the loose box, Steph tensed.
Judy was going to see her with Comet at
any moment!

In an attempt to hide the magic pony, she shot outside, closed the door, and stood with her back pressed against it. Comet seemed to think it was some kind of game and leaned over her shoulder to nuzzle her hair.

"There you are!" Judy said, smiling. "What's so interesting about that empty box? I thought you'd have chosen a pony and tacked it up by now."

Empty box? Steph could feel Comet's warm breath tickling her neck. But, for some reason, Judy didn't seem to be able to see him.

"I have used my magic, so that only you can see and hear me," Comet whinnied softly in her ear.

"Oh!" Steph just about managed not to jump out of her skin. "Oh, right. Cool!"

She gave Judy a huge cheesy grin. "I
mean . . . um . . . The ponies are all cool.
I can't decide which one to ride." She
pointed hastily toward a large gray pony
in the nearest box. "I . . . um . . . think
I'd like to ride that one, please."

"Good choice," Judy said, grinning at
her enthusiasm. "Misty's just the right size
for you. You'll find her very responsive.
I'll show you where her tack is."

Steph followed Judy into the tack
room and emerged a few moments later
carrying a saddle, with a bridle looped
over her arm. Judy had led the gray pony
out and secured her to a metal ring in
the wall.

As Steph began tacking up Misty,
Judy stood by. She nodded with approval.
"You seem to know what you're doing."

"I started riding when I was five years old," Steph said. She caught a movement from the corner of her eye and only just managed to suppress a gasp. Comet's head was pushing through the loose-box door. His neck, front legs, and the rest of him followed and then he stood waiting calmly, while Steph buckled on her riding hat and mounted Misty.

She wasn't sure whether to laugh or pinch herself to see if she was dreaming.

Judy hadn't noticed anything unusual. "You can take Misty along the bridle path that leads down to the canal. Do you know it?"

Steph nodded. "I used to ride Fleur, my old pony, along that path beside the canal. It's a great ride." She felt a wave of sadness as she thought again about riding Fleur.

"Yes, it is," Judy agreed. "You'll know the pedestrian bridge then. Cross over the canal there and then come back to the stables. Okay?"

"All right. Thanks, Judy. See you later." Steph patted the gray mare's neck as she used her heels to nudge her forward.

As she, Misty, and Comet trotted out of the stable yard and headed for the bridle path, Steph smiled to herself.

She was glad that her dad had
persuaded her to try out the new riding
stables in an attempt to cheer her up.
She hadn't forgotten about Fleur, like he
seemed to hope she would, but Steph had
a sneaking suspicion that this amazing
magic pony might turn out to be a very
special friend!

Chapter THREE

Misty was a smooth ride, and Steph relaxed in the saddle as she continued along the bridle path with Comet at her side. The sky was bright blue, and bees buzzed among the colorful wildflowers that dotted the grass on either side.

Comet looked around, scanning the countryside with keen bright eyes for any sign of Destiny. Steph peered into

the bushes and hedges as they passed,
keeping her eyes open, too.

The bridle path followed the curve
of a valley on its way down to the canal.
There were fields of bright yellow flowers
on one side. A bit farther on, they passed
acres of dusty-green ripening corn and
then came to some clumps of trees.

Comet saw a movement in a thicket
of birches and galloped off to investigate.

Steph halted Misty. She was deciding whether to leave the path and follow him when Comet appeared through the trees and came back toward her.

"It was only someone walking their dog," he told her sadly.

Steph could see that his deep-violet eyes were shadowed by disappointment. "I'm sorry you didn't find Destiny," she said gently. "But there are lots of other places to look."

Comet nodded, and his black mane swung forward. "At least I can be sure that Destiny did not pass by this way."

"How can you know that?" Steph asked curiously.

"Destiny and I have a special bond because we are twins. If she is close, I will sense her presence. Also, if she has passed by at any time, she will have left a trail."

"Do you mean like broken stalks and stuff?" Steph guessed.

"No. There will be dimly glowing hoofprints, which are invisible to most people in your world."

"Will I be able to see them?"

"Only if you are riding with me or we are very close," Comet told her. "I think because you are special enough to see me that you will be able to see Destiny's hoofprints, too."

Steph smiled. She was growing very fond of Comet.

The magic pony pawed at the grass with one front hoof. "Are you ready to go on, Steph? I would like to keep searching."

"Sure. Let's go!" Steph squeezed Misty, letting her know she was ready to move on.

They reached the part of the track that led to the canal. Steph turned Misty onto the old path. Comet followed, his mane and tail stirring in the warm breeze.

Brightly painted houseboats with cheerful rose and castle designs were moored alongside the canal. Some of them had window boxes and pots filled with red and orange flowers. Longer black barges slid through the greenish water. People called out and waved as Steph rode along.

Steph waved back, feeling a surge
of happiness. It was a perfect day for
doing what she loved best in the whole
world. Riding! Especially with the magic
pony who had chosen her to be his
special friend.

They passed fields and then some
buildings and a yard filled with lorries.
Some time later, they rounded a bend.
"There's the bridge," Steph said, pointing
ahead. "We have to go across it."

Comet pricked his ears eagerly. "It
looks high up."

Steph nodded. "It is. You can see a
long way from up there."

The bridge was very old, with painted
cast-iron railings. Misty's hooves clip-
clopped on the wooden boards, but
Comet's made no sound.

"I can't see any ponies in the fields, can you?" Steph asked Comet as they paused in the middle to look out over the canal.

"No, I cannot." Comet turned his head to look toward the marina on one side, where the masts of many sailing boats seemed to prick the sky. In the other direction were houses and a dark-green forest behind them. His eyes lit up with interest as he looked at the thick trees. "That would be a good place for Destiny to hide," he neighed.

"I'm supposed to go back to the stables now," Steph said. "But I could try to sneak out and meet you later, and then we can go and look together."

Comet nodded. "You could ride on my back. We would travel more quickly that way."

"Oh wow. Really?" Steph felt a thrill
at the thought of riding the magic pony.
She was surprised to realize that she
couldn't wait.

They picked up the bridle path again

after crossing the bridge. As the riding stables came into view, Steph had a sudden thought.

"Where are you going to stay?" she asked Comet. "You can't live at the riding stables. They'll probably put another pony in that empty box."

Comet flicked one ear as he turned to look at her. "You are right, Steph. I will come home with you," he decided.

"Really? Oh, I'd love that," Steph cried. "You can stay in Fleur's old stable." Steph was sure that Fleur wouldn't have minded. "It's perfect! And I can spend tons of time with you and we can go out looking for Destiny together—" She broke off as she realized there was a snag in her plan. "Except that I don't see how I can get you to our house. You don't know the way. And you can't gallop behind the car, it's too dangerous. I know! I'll call Dad and tell him I'm walking home. It's not that far. Then I can ride you."

Comet nodded, looking pleased.

"It's settled then," Steph said happily.

But as she reached the stable's parking lot, she groaned. "Oh no! Too late. There's our car."

Mr. Danes saw her riding. He got out of the car and stood waiting as she rode Misty into the yard. "Hi, Steph!" he called, waving.

Steph forced a smile as she waved back. "Now what are we going to do?" she murmured, looking sideways at Comet.

The magic pony flicked his tail and gave her a mysterious smile. She felt faint tingles flowing down her fingers. Before she could ask what was going on, her magic pony had disappeared, leaving only the tiniest shower of violet sparks.

Chapter
FOUR

"So did you have a good time?" Steph's
dad wanted to know as they drove home.

"Yes, thanks. It was . . . um . . . great.
Judy was really friendly and Misty's a great
pony," Steph said, mustering up all the
enthusiasm she could. It had been really
kind of her dad to arrange the surprise
for her, and she didn't want to seem
ungrateful. His plan had worked in a way;

she was starting to feel better about not having Fleur around. But now she was worried about Comet. Where had he gone so suddenly?

Maybe she would never see him again.

He's probably changed his mind about coming home with me and decided to look for his twin sister all by himself from now on, she thought glumly.

Steph shifted uncomfortably in her seat. A lump in her jeans pocket was pressing into her leg. What could it be? She didn't remember putting a tissue or anything in there. Puzzled, she slipped her hand into the pocket and felt her fingers close around something very small and soft.

Steph drew the tiny object out and her eyes widened in surprise as she saw what she was holding. It was a miniature soft toy pony. As she gazed at it, the fluffy little black-and-white pony shook itself and blinked at her with bead-bright violet eyes.

"Comet!" She gasped, and then quickly turned it into sneeze. "Ah-choo!"

"Bless you," her dad said.

Comet stretched his neck to look up at her. "I found another way of coming home with you!" he told Steph in a miniature neigh that matched his new size.

She smiled down at him delightedly. Comet was unbelievably beautiful as his real winged self, and handsome as a black-and-white pony—but right now he was the sweetest, most gorgeous fluffy miniature pony she had ever seen.

Her dad looked back at her for a second. "Cute toy. Did Judy give you that?" he asked.

Steph thought fast. "Um . . . yeah! They're giving them to all the new customers. It's to . . . um . . . to help advertise the new stables," she improvised.

Her dad nodded slowly. "That's a great idea. Very enterprising."

Steph realized that Comet's magic must be working again; making sure that only she could see that the tiny toy was alive.

The moment she got home, Steph said a quick hello to her mom and then made an excuse about having to clean some of Fleur's tack. She rushed straight outside to the stable. Once there, she gently put Comet on the floor, where he seemed even tinier in the empty stall.

Steph felt a stronger warm tingling flow to the very tips of her fingers. The toy horse's black-and-white fur glittered with miniature sparkles like violet fairy lights. A faint rainbow mist spread outward, and suddenly Comet appeared as a normal-size black-and-white pony.

Steph went forward and threw her arms around his neck. "That was amazing! You're full of surprises!" she said, laying

her cheek against his warm, satiny skin. "I'm so glad you decided to come home with me. I think it's best if you stay invisible, so Mom or Dad don't see you and ask awkward questions."

Comet gave a soft, contented blow. "I think so, too."

As Steph lowered her arms and stood back, Comet raised his head and swiveled his ears. He peered intently toward the open door.

"What is it?" she asked him, turning to look down the side of the house. From here she had a restricted view of the cul-de-sac.

"I hear hoofbeats approaching," he told her in an urgent little neigh.

"But I'm the only person in Porlock Close who owned a pony." Steph caught

her breath as a thought struck her. "What
if it's Destiny? Maybe *she's* found *you!*"

"I do hope so! I have missed her
so much." Comet's eyes glowed like
amethysts. He trotted outside eagerly.

Steph followed more slowly. If it *was*
Destiny, maybe Comet would take her
straight back with him to Rainbow Mist
Island. She felt a pang as she realized that
she'd barely gotten used to having Comet
for a friend. She certainly wasn't ready to
lose him so soon.

As Steph and Comet reached the front
drive, a girl on a stunning dark bay pony
rode up to them.

Comet's head drooped slightly, and
his eyes lost a little of their color. "That is
not Destiny," he whinnied sadly.

"I'm sorry you're disappointed," Steph

said soothingly, feeling guilty at her sense of relief that he would be staying with her. "Don't forget we're going to check out those woods we saw from the canal bridge."

Comet nodded, his eyes glistening with renewed hope.

The girl drew her pony to a halt. "Hi! Found you at last!" she said with a friendly smile. She looked at Steph, unable to see Comet, who stood next to her. "I've noticed you riding past our house a few times on your chestnut pony and wanted to meet you. I don't know anyone else around here who owns a pony. I'm Ellie Browning."

"Hi, Ellie," Steph said. "I'm Stephanie Danes, but everyone calls me Steph." She looked admiringly at the elegant bay.

"Your pony's gorgeous. What's his name?"

"Turpin," Ellie said proudly, tossing back the long dark-red hair that streamed out from under her riding hat. "He's an Arab. I haven't had him that long."

"Hello, Turpin." Steph held out her hand, so the pony could get her scent. He was the color of strong coffee, and his mane and tail were almost black.

"Would you like to come over to my house?" Ellie invited. "We can put the ponies through their paces. It'll be fun. We've just moved into the old house near the village green."

Steph knew that Ellie was referring to Fleur, as she couldn't see Comet. She tried not to feel too sad and she hoped the little chestnut was settling in with her new owner.

She knew Ellie's house. It was very large, with a stone porch and pillars beside the red front door. A row of small trees, clipped into triangles, lined the smart drive. There were usually expensive cars parked there.

"I'd love to come, but I don't have a pony now." *At least, not one I can tell you about*, she thought. "I just had to sell

Fleur. I got too big for her," she told Ellie.

"Oh, that's a shame. You must miss her," Ellie said sympathetically. "Turpin's my first pony. At my old house, I always rode riding-school ponies. But we've got a lot of space now, so Mom and Dad bought me my very own pony. Why don't you come over anyway? We can take turns riding Turpin."

Steph smiled, liking Ellie more and more. She hoped they would become friends. She felt excited by the idea of riding the little Arab pony. "I'd love to. When should I come over?"

Ellie put her head on one side. "Let's see. Tomorrow's Sunday, so I have to visit my grandma, who lives hours away. How about Monday? It's a holiday, so we can have the whole day together."

"Great!" Steph said.

They decided on a time, and then Steph stood by as Ellie clicked her tongue at Turpin and squeezed him on. Steph watched until they rode out of Porlock Close.

"She seems really nice, doesn't she?" Steph said to Comet.

"I liked her, too."

Steph thought he sounded a little sad after the false alarm and was probably

thinking about his missing twin. She reached up to pat his shoulder as they walked back to the stable, promising herself that she'd get up extra early the following morning so they could go out searching for Destiny.

Chapter
FIVE

Sunday morning dawned bright and clear.

It was only just light when Steph woke and put on her jeans and T-shirt quickly. Dashing downstairs, she grabbed her riding boots and hat from the utility room and then hurried outside to the stable.

Comet whinnied a soft welcome as soon as he saw her.

"Are you ready to go? I think we have a couple of hours before Mom and Dad get up. We can check out those woods we saw from the canal bridge."

The magic pony pushed his velvety nose into her hand, his deep-violet eyes sparkling with affection. "Thank you, Steph. Climb onto my back."

Steph mounted. She twined her hands in Comet's thick mane as he leaped forward and galloped down the side of the house.

The streets were calm and almost empty. Comet sped along, his hooves making no sound on the pavement. He was exciting to ride and as fast as the wind.

Steph bit back a gasp of excitement as she crouched low on his back. Houses, shops, the canal, and hedges all whooshed past in a sparkly blur, and then they were out in the open countryside.

Faster, ever faster, Comet raced. His magic seemed to spread over Steph like a warm cloak, and she felt safe and secure astride him—almost as if she was surrounded by a protective bubble of rainbow magic. Comet slowed his pace as they entered the woods and began to weave along the paths through the trees.

Steph looked from left to right, searching for evidence that a pony might have taken cover there, but there was no sign of Destiny or any trace of glowing hoofprints.

Comet stretched his neck and raked the bushes and tangles of undergrowth with his keen eyes.

After carefully searching every inch of the woods, they had to admit defeat.

"The morning mist has dried and the sun is high in the sky," Comet pointed out to Steph as they stood at the top of a steep bank. "I will take you back now."

Steph could have gone on riding Comet for hours. "Okay." She patted his neck reassuringly. Steph knew that her mom and dad would be getting up soon anyway. "We can go out searching again tomorrow, when we go over to Ellie's house."

Comet wheeled around and was about to retrace his steps when a gust of wind came out of nowhere. Suddenly, a white plastic bag flew out of a bush and wrapped around his front legs. With a squeal of alarm, Comet reared up, kicking out and trying to dislodge the scary thing he thought was attacking him.

"Oh!" Taken by surprise, Steph lost her grip on his mane. She slid down his back and luckily managed to land on her feet.

"It's okay, Comet. It's only a bag. It won't hurt you!" she cried.

In his panic Comet didn't seem to hear

her. He snorted and edged backward until
he was in danger of slipping down the
side of the bank.

He would hurt himself if he fell!
Steph thought fast. Grabbing a tree
branch from the ground, she dashed
beneath his flailing hooves and hooked
the plastic bag with the twig.

"Yes!" she cried, as she pulled it free,
bundled it up, and stuffed it into her jeans
pocket.

But as Steph took a step back, she stumbled and felt herself falling.

"Oh!" She tumbled over and over down the slope. One of her arms hit a large stone, and pain shot through her.

Biting her lip, Steph struggled to her feet, quickly climbed back up, and then staggered over to sit on a fallen log. To her relief, Comet seemed unharmed.

The magic pony's sides heaved as he gradually calmed down. He looked around for Steph and walked over to where she was sitting. Leaning down, he gently snuffled her shoulder, surrounding her with sweet hay-scented breath.

"Thank you, Steph. It was very brave of you to help me."

"I couldn't bear it if anything happened to you. I thought you were going to tumble down that bank," she said. "Oh!" she gasped, holding her numb arm. Now that the excitement was over, it was beginning to throb painfully.

"You are hurt!" Comet said. "I will help you."

He blew out another warm breath. This time it twinkled with a million tiny violet stars. The sparkly healing mist swirled around Steph's arm for a few moments before it sank into it and disappeared. She felt the pain in her numb arm increase a little before suddenly draining away like water gurgling down a drain.

"Oh, thank you, Comet. I feel much better!" she said, stroking the broad white stripe on his nose.

"Good." He snorted affectionately. "I am glad to be able to take care of you. And

I will always do so while I am here."

Steph looked up at him adoringly. "I hope you'll live here with me forever. And there's room for Destiny, too. You could both stay."

"That is not possible," Comet neighed softly. "We must return to our family on Rainbow Mist Island. Do you understand that, Steph?"

Steph nodded slowly, feeling her chest tighten with sadness.

She realized how fond of him she'd become. Comet had gradually filled the space left in her heart by Fleur. The thought of one day losing him was too painful to think about. She decided not to dwell on that now and, instead, to enjoy every single moment she could.

Comet whickered and reached out to

nudge her arm gently. "Climb onto me again, Steph,"

She mounted and he sprang forward. The journey home was even faster. Time seemed almost to stand still, and then Steph was beside the magic pony again in the stable. "I'll come out and see you later," she promised, before hurrying into the house.

She was pouring cereal into a bowl for breakfast in the kitchen when she heard her mom coming down the stairs.

"Hello, sweetie!" Mrs. Danes said, blinking in surprise as she walked over to turn the coffeemaker on. "Why are you up so early?"

You'd never believe me, even if I could tell you! Steph thought, biting back a secret grin. "Oh, no reason really. I just couldn't sleep in on such a beautiful day!" she said casually.

Chapter
SIX

Steph set out early on Comet to
ride over and see Ellie at her house the
following day. Comet's magic made sure
that they were invisible to everyone for
the whole ride.

As Steph had promised him, they
took the opportunity to check out the
village streets for signs of Destiny, but
there was still no trace of Comet's twin

sister. Steph dismounted at the back of the quiet churchyard, and then Comet walked invisibly beside her as she called for Ellie.

Mrs. Browning opened the door. "Hello, you must be Steph. Nice to meet you."

"Hello, Mrs. Browning," Steph said politely.

"Ellie told me that you just had to sell your pony. That's a shame."

"I know. I really miss her," Steph told Ellie's mom, feeling a lump rise in her throat. "I had Fleur for three years, but she went to a really good home." She took a deep breath and quickly changed the subject. "Ellie seems thrilled with Turpin. He's a gorgeous pony."

"Yes, he is. Ellie loves him to pieces. I'm not sure that she quite understands what looking after him involves yet, though. I suspect most girls are like that with their first ponies."

"I guess some are," Steph agreed. "I always loved everything about looking after ponies and horses. I want to work with them when I grow up."

"Good for you. Perhaps you can give

Ellie a few tips. She's with Turpin now. I'll
open the side gate so you can walk down
the garden to the stable." Mrs. Browning
came outside and Steph followed her.

The back garden was enormous, with
tennis courts, a summer house, and a
swimming pool. The stable was on the
other side. It was an impressive redbrick
building beside a large paddock.

"Wow! Just look at this place," Steph
whispered to Comet, her eyes widening.

Comet glanced around. "It is very
nice here. But I like my stable at the place
where you live."

"I'm glad, because I love having you
living with me!" Steph threw him an
adoring look.

"Hi, Steph!" Ellie appeared at the
stable door. She wore a blue T-shirt with

a designer pony logo, jodhpurs, and boots. "Come on in."

Inside the stable, Steph caught her breath. There was room here for two ponies. Another door led to a tack room and feed store, with a counter and a deep sink. Yet another door led to a toilet with a washbasin.

Steph shaped her lips into a silent whistle. "This is like a palace!" It would be a dream to keep a pony in a place like this.

Ellie smiled. "I know. I'm really lucky to have it. Mom says that Dad got a bit carried away when he had it built."

Steph laughed.

She hoped again that they might become good friends. It would be fun for her and Comet to spend time with Ellie and Turpin.

Turpin was in one of the stalls. His ears twitched inquisitively, and he turned his supple neck to look at them.

"Hello, beautiful," Steph said. He really was a good-looking pony. She loved Arabs; they had such elegant heads and big soft eyes.

As she went closer to pat him, she frowned. There were traces of dried mud

on his legs and bits of twig and grass in his
tail. His bay coat was a bit dull, too.

Steph's fingers itched for her grooming
kit. She would love to be let loose on
Turpin. She imagined untangling his
mane and tail and spraying conditioner on
them, before brushing his entire coffee-
colored coat until it was smooth and
glossy.

"Oh, Turpin," Ellie scolded gently.
"You haven't touched your new hay net.
You're not feeling all moody, are you?"

Steph glanced into the stall and
immediately saw that the hay net had
been hung up too high and Turpin was
straining to reach it.

"You need to bring the net down a bit,
so he can get to it more easily," she said
without thinking. "Ponies can get grass

seeds in their eyes with the net above them."

Ellie reddened. "I knew that," she snapped, going into the stall to adjust it.

Steph bit her lip. She remembered what Mrs. Browning had said about Ellie not being all that used to the hard work of looking after a pony. Maybe it would be best to go easy with the advice.

But she couldn't help noticing a heap of bridles lying in a tangle on the floor. Two expensive horse blankets had been dumped in a corner, despite the blanket box standing open.

Comet blew air from his nostrils and wrinkled his lips at the slight tang of soiled straw.

"Yes, I can smell it, too," Steph whispered to him. "I don't think Ellie realizes that you have to do regular poo picking." She turned to Ellie. "Where do you keep your fork and skip? I'll give you a hand to pick up those fresh droppings. I know it's a bit boring having to do it all the time. But it's one of those things you can't get out of." She rolled her eyes, as if she found it a chore, too.

"Tell me about it!" Ellie said with feeling as she led Turpin out of his stall.

"I didn't realize how much hard work it was to look after your own pony. Mom and Dad say that Turpin's my responsibility, so I have to learn to do it by myself." She sighed. "Anyway, leave those droppings for now. I'll clean them up later before I get Turpin in for the night. Let's go and have some fun with him. Aren't you dying to ride him?"

"You bet!" Steph said, deciding not to nag about cleaning up, in case Ellie got annoyed again. Anyway, she was really excited to try out her new friend's Arab pony.

Ellie put Turpin into the paddock and Steph and Comet followed them in.

The magic pony immediately cantered across the grass and then lay down. Snorting happily, Comet rolled onto his back, all four legs waving in the air.

Steph hid a smile, pleased that Comet was enjoying himself.

With an eager nicker, Turpin trotted over and sniffed Comet curiously. Comet got to his feet and shook himself, his dark mane flying outward. He reached out and snuffled Turpin's neck.

Steph watched delightedly as the ponies got acquainted. Maybe Comet wouldn't miss Destiny so much if he made a new pony friend.

Kicking up their heels, Turpin and Comet cantered down to the other side of the paddock and then stood side by side, cropping the grass.

Ellie frowned. "He's never gone rushing off like that before. Come here, Turpin! Come on, boy!" she encouraged.

Turpin twitched his ears. He looked toward Ellie and then lowered his head again.

Ellie sighed and began stomping toward him. Turpin eyed her. He waited until she got within a couple of feet and then danced away with his tail jinked up in the air.

Ellie stopped, waiting until her pony began to crop the grass again before advancing. The same thing happened. Turpin stayed where he was until Ellie was almost within reach, then flicked his tail up and shot away again.

Steph laughed, guessing that this could go on for some time.

"Hey! It's not funny!" Ellie cried, annoyed. "Dumb pony! What's wrong with him today?"

"He's just being silly!" Steph said. *And showing off in front of Comet!* "I could show you a trick to get him to come to you, if you like."

Ellie looked intrigued. "Go on."

Steph moved forward a few paces. She

waved her arms in the air to get Turpin's attention. When he looked at her, she turned her back. Crouching down, she pretended to be looking at something in the grass.

"Wow! Look at this," she said enthusiastically.

"What's there? I can't see anything," Ellie said.

"That's because there's nothing there! But Turpin doesn't know that. He won't be able to resist coming over to see what I'm doing," Steph explained, chancing a furtive look over her shoulder.

She saw Turpin's ears twitch forward. He snorted softly and took a few steps forward.

"It's working!" Ellie whispered as the little Arab pony kept coming.

Steph waited until Turpin stopped and stretched his neck toward her. Very slowly, she reached up and took hold of his head collar, at the same time rising smoothly to her feet.

"Clever boy," she praised, rubbing his satiny cheek.

Ellie looked impressed. "That's a neat trick. I'd never have thought of that. How come you know so much about ponies?"

Steph was glad that Ellie seemed to have calmed down a bit with her. "I love learning new stuff. I'm weird like that!" she joked modestly. "Is it okay if we ride Turpin now?"

"Sure. Go for it. You first," Ellie said generously.

Steph swung herself up. The Arab pony was just the right size for her. She settled herself comfortably, urging Turpin into a trot and then a canter. He had a smooth, even stride and was alert and responsive to her commands.

"Turpin's a dream to ride. He's exactly the sort of pony I'd like next," she said to Ellie as she dismounted. "He's so sweet-natured and intelligent. Are you going to show him?"

"I might. I haven't decided yet," Ellie said evasively.

Steph widened her eyes. "Oh, you totally have to! He's a real winner!" she enthused.

"I think so, too!" Ellie said, smiling, but then she wrinkled her nose. "But it's a bit of a sore point right now. My parents won't let me enter any competitions until I'm better at taking care of Turpin. Can you believe that?"

Steph knew not to say anything. From the little she'd already seen, she thought Ellie had some way to go before her parents felt that she was a competent pony owner. But she didn't want to say so, in case Ellie got defensive with her again.

Ellie had mounted Turpin and was riding him around the paddock. Steph watched, impressed. There was nothing

wrong with Ellie's riding skills. She
was confident, perfectly in control, and
sensitive to her mount.

Ellie's face was glowing as she cantered
back to where Steph was waiting.

"Isn't he incredible?" she said, leaning
over to pat her pony's neck.

"He certainly is," Steph agreed
admiringly.

Then it was her turn to ride Turpin
again.

At the end of the afternoon, Steph
was feeling relaxed and full of the
afterglow of a few hours of enjoyable
riding. As Ellie went to lead her pony
back to his stable, she made a suggestion.

"Why don't we leave both ponies in
the paddock and I'll help you do Turpin's
bedding and clear things up?"

A puzzled look crossed Ellie's face.
"Ponies? There's only one in the paddock!
Unless one of them is invisible!"

"Oh yeah! Silly me!" Steph said
quickly, glancing at Comet, who was
cheekily flicking one ear toward her. "It
must be wishful thinking. I guess I'm
still missing Fleur! So, about Turpin's
bedding . . ."

Ellie sighed deeply. "Don't you start bossing me around, too! It's bad enough having Mom and Dad always at me!" she grumbled.

"I wasn't . . . I wouldn't . . . !" Steph countered, feeling herself starting to get annoyed at last. She'd done all she could to be friendly, but Ellie seemed determined to take everything the wrong way. "I guess I should go then. See you later," she called out shortly as she walked away.

There was no answer from Ellie.

Chapter
SEVEN

"How did you get along with Ellie?"
Steph's dad asked that evening as they sat
around the table having dinner.

"We had a . . . um . . . good time,"
Steph said. She was already regretting
leaving so abruptly. "I enjoyed riding
Turpin. He's a really nice pony. I think
we're going to meet up again tomorrow
afternoon near the woods behind her

house." *At least I hope we are*, she thought, *unless Ellie is still mad at me.*

"Lucky you. I'm glad you've found a new friend with a pony. Especially one who lives nearby," her mom commented.

They finished eating, and Steph helped clear away the dishes. There were some bits of apple and carrot left over from the salad. Without thinking, she slipped them into her pocket for Comet.

Her dad raised his eyebrows at her in surprise.

"I . . . um . . . might need a snack later," Steph said hurriedly. "At least it's better than eating sweets."

"Maybe I should follow your lead," her dad said, patting his round tummy.

Mrs. Danes laughed. "Well, it wouldn't hurt you. Just kidding!" she said as her husband grimaced. She looked at Steph. "I know you're still missing Fleur, but I wondered whether we should start looking for a bigger and more challenging pony for you. What do you think?"

Steph considered this carefully. Was she ready to look for another pony to take the little chestnut's place? Did she even want a brand-new pony to look after and love, now that she had Comet in her life?

But Steph knew that Comet was also a Lightning Horse who lived in another world and could never belong to her— not like a pony of her own.

She made a decision. "Okay, but if I have a new pony, I'd like one just like Turpin. Everything about him is great."

"I got a brief glimpse of Ellie on the front drive. That little Arab's a stunner, all right," her dad agreed. "I can see why you're so taken with him. But I'm not sure we can afford a pony of his breeding right now."

"That's okay. I don't mind waiting," Steph said helpfully. *Perfect!* she thought. It would probably give her time to get used to the idea of riding a new pony.

Her mom looked surprised. "Are you sure? It might take us a while to save up."

"No problem! I can always go to the riding school. They have some really nice ponies," Steph replied.

"And maybe Ellie will let you ride Turpin now and then," her dad added.

Steph said nothing. She wasn't so sure about that. She and Ellie weren't exactly getting along.

But her parents seemed happy with their decision. So it was settled.

Once her mom had left for her monthly book group and her dad was tinkering about in the garden shed, Steph slipped outside to give Comet his treats.

He crunched up the apple and carrots with his strong teeth. "Delicious! Thank you, Steph."

"You're welcome." She threaded her fingers through his thick black mane,

stroking it flat as she told him about the
conversation with her mom and dad.
"I hope we get to meet up with Ellie
and Turpin again, don't you?" she said
wistfully.

Comet nodded, chewing.

"Ellie might not want to be friends with me now. She thinks I boss her around, like her parents. But I only wanted to help. There's a lot to learn about when you get your first pony." She sighed. "I wish I knew how to make her like me again."

"You will find a way, Steph," Comet neighed confidently.

Steph leaned forward and Comet cantered along. Her fingers tingled slightly as his warm magic swirled around her again. They were on their way to meet Ellie and Turpin near the woods—hopefully.

Despite worrying about whether Ellie would show up, Steph felt a burst

of pure happiness. Riding Comet was
so wonderful. She knew she'd never get
bored of it.

They soon reached the wooded area.
Wide paths wound among the birches and
field maples, and there was a flat grassed
area with a shallow pond in the center.

Steph looked around, but she couldn't
see Ellie and Turpin. She didn't mind if
they were late. It meant she would have
longer to ride Comet before she had to
find somewhere out of sight to dismount
and become visible again.

Comet moved along a grass path, bars
of sunlight and shade striping his smooth
patched coat.

"It's really pretty here, isn't it? Oh!"
Steph gasped.

She only just managed to keep from

slipping sideways as Comet came to
a sudden halt. He stretched his neck
forward to snuffle at the ground.

"Comet? What's going on?" She
glanced down to see a faint line of softly
glowing violet hoofprints. They led
between the trees and stretched away into
the distance.

"Destiny! She has been here!" Comet
neighed joyfully.

Did that mean that Comet was leaving to go after her? "Is she close? Can you tell where she is?" Steph asked him anxiously.

Comet shook his head. "The trail is cold. But I know now that Destiny came this way. When I am very close to catching up with her, I will be able to hear her hoofbeats. And then I may have to leave suddenly, without saying good-bye."

"Oh." Steph felt a tug of dismay as she realized that she would never be ready to lose her magical friend. "Are you sure that you and Destiny wouldn't like to stay here and live with me?" she asked in a small voice.

Comet shook his head, his eyes softening. "We must return to our family on Rainbow Mist Island," he reminded her gently.

Steph nodded sadly. "Destiny must be missing her home after being lost for so long." Her eyes stung with tears, but she knew that she must face the truth, however hard it was. Besides, Comet wasn't leaving yet. There was still time to enjoy every moment spent with him.

She saw something from the corner of her eye as a pony and rider approached the woods. It was Ellie and Turpin.

Comet quickly slipped behind a thick bush, and Steph slid from his back. There was a tiny spurt of violet sparkles as she became visible again.

Steph stepped out and began walking toward Ellie. "Hi! Ellie! I'm over here!" she called delightedly.

"Steph!" Ellie called, a note of
urgency in her voice. She encouraged
Turpin into a trot. "I . . . I'm sorry I was
a pain yesterday. Can we still be friends?"

"You bet!" Steph said happily.

She frowned as they rode up. Turpin
looked a bit strange. She couldn't see
why, until Ellie reined him in.

Turpin had just been clipped. Cutting
the pony's coat using electric clippers
was something only experienced owners
attempted.

Steph had never seen such a botched
job. A good clip left smooth skin and
neat areas of unclipped longer coat. Poor
Turpin had random wobbly lines cut
through his coat on his sides and back.

"Oh my goodness! Who did that?"
Steph asked, horrified.

Ellie's face said it all.

"*You* did it? But why?" Steph
blinked at her friend in amazement. She
couldn't believe that Ellie had attempted
something so complicated.

Ellie rolled her eyes. "Mom and
Dad were bugging me *again* about how
I had to learn how to look after Turpin

properly. So I thought I'd impress them by giving him a clip. I read how to do it in one of my pony magazines, and it looked really easy. But I couldn't get it to look right. Then the clippers went blunt and I couldn't find the spare blades."

"Well, you can't leave him like that," Steph said, aghast. "It looks like moths have been chomping him!"

Ellie's face fell. "If you're just going to make fun—"

"I'm not," Steph cut in quickly, wishing that she'd bitten her tongue. Ellie was obviously upset, although trying hard not to show it, and she didn't want them to fall out again. Especially since they'd only just made up after last time. "Um . . . is there anything I can do to help?"

"Yes. You can clip him properly for me," Ellie stated.

"What!" Steph looked at her in horror. Clipping a pony was really complicated and could take ages. "I helped while Fleur was clipped once, so I know what to do. But I don't think I'm up to doing the whole thing by myself."

"You have to try! Please!" Ellie begged. "Mom and Dad are out, but they'll be back soon. They'll go nuts if they see Turpin looking like this."

Steph felt squeezed into a corner. She guessed that Ellie wasn't exaggerating; she was already on thin ice with her parents where Turpin was concerned.

"Well—okay then," Steph decided reluctantly. "I'll just have to do my best.

I'll get my grooming kit and meet you at your house."

Ellie beamed at her in relief. "Thanks, Steph. You'll be as quick as you can, right?"

"Okay." Steph let out a sigh of exasperation as Ellie rode away. "I must be crazy. It's going to take a miracle to make Turpin look even half decent. That's if I even have time to get started before Ellie's mom and dad see him!"

"I will help you," Comet neighed.

"Thanks, Comet. What would I do without you?" Steph smiled gratefully at her magical friend.

Chapter EIGHT

As soon as Ellie couldn't see her, Steph mounted Comet and held on tightly. Rainbow streaks glittered in the magic pony's flowing black mane and tail as he galloped at the speed of light toward Steph's house. They picked up the plastic box with her grooming kit and clippers and quickly set off back to Ellie's before Steph's mom and dad realized she'd been there.

On arriving at Ellie's, Comet's
shining hooves barely brushed the
ground as he galloped into the paddock
behind the stable and stopped for Steph
to dismount.

Steph immediately became visible
and ran toward the stable door. Comet
followed by her side. They had only

taken a few steps when they heard raised voices.

Steph caught her breath in alarm. "Uh-oh! It sounds like Ellie's mom and dad have come back early," she whispered.

Mr. Browning's angry voice floated out of the open door. "Honestly, Ellie. Look at this place. There's stuff lying about everywhere. Turpin's kicked over his water bucket and doesn't have anything to drink."

"I . . . um . . . haven't had time to clean it up. I was just going to, but—" Ellie burst out.

"No more excuses," Mrs. Browning said firmly. "I think we have to accept that you're not ready to own a pony. You'd be better off going back to riding-school ponies for a while."

"No! I am ready. I know I am," Ellie insisted. "Please let me keep Turpin! I couldn't bear it if you sold him. I love him so much!"

"I know that, honey. No one's arguing about that," her mom said gently.

"Loving a pony isn't enough, I'm afraid," Ellie's dad added. "You have to accept the responsibility of taking care of one, too. I agree with your mom about this."

Steph chewed at her lip. Poor Ellie was getting a severe scolding. What could she do? She knew in her heart that Ellie had what it took to be a good pony owner. She could see that she loved Turpin almost as much as Steph loved Comet! Steph really wanted to help Ellie discover that for herself, but she might never get the chance to do that now.

On impulse, she stepped forward and
rushed straight into the stable.

The atmosphere inside was electric.

Ellie stood there facing her furious
parents with hunched shoulders. Her hands
were thrust into her jeans pockets. Tears
were trickling down her face.

Only Turpin was calm, placidly
pulling at his hay net with soft ripping and

chewing noises. The wobbly lines cut into his coat looked even worse in the sunshine pouring in through an overhead window.

"Hi, Ellie," Steph said breezily. "I sharpened my clippers and found the spare blades. So I can finish with Turpin's clip—oh . . . er . . . hi," she said. She looked around with wide eyes at Ellie's parents, as if she'd only just noticed that there was something wrong.

"Steph?" Mrs. Browning frowned. "*You* clipped Turpin?"

Steph nodded. "Um . . . yeah. I made a bit of a mess, didn't I? Sorry. I was hoping to clean him up before you saw him." She gave what she hoped was a convincingly guilty shrug.

Ellie's dad raised his eyebrows as he

turned to his daughter. "Ellie? Why didn't you tell us this?"

Ellie opened and closed her mouth. She wiped her wet eyes with the back of her hands as she threw a puzzled glance at Steph.

Steph took a deep breath and plunged in. "She probably didn't want to get me into trouble. Ellie didn't want me to clip Turpin, but I did it anyway. I s'pose I was showing off," she lied. "And then it all went wrong because my clippers were blunt."

"Well, at least you're honest," Mrs. Browning said tersely. "But it was a very irresponsible thing to do."

"I know. And I am really sorry," Steph repeated. She hung her head, not caring how much hot water she got into if it was going to help Ellie keep Turpin. "Especially since I knew Ellie would be in a lot of trouble if you saw Turpin looking so awful—even if it wasn't her fault." She had a sudden idea. "So that's why I've promised to . . . give Ellie a hand with mucking out and stuff."

Ellie was stunned. "Um . . . you have?

Steph gave her a level look, pleading with her eyes for Ellie to go along with this. "Definitely. Remember? We agreed that I'd come over every day and help you get into a good routine with Turpin. I'm going to show you how to groom him, too, and pick out his hooves, aren't I?"

Ellie blinked at her, catching on at last. "That's right. We . . . um . . . only just arranged it. I haven't had time to tell you yet," she said to her parents.

Mr. Browning ran his hand through his hair. He grinned drily. "Well, I guess your mom and I didn't give you much of a chance to speak up. We did kind of barge right in. Maybe we were a bit hasty to talk about selling Turpin. What do you think?" he asked, looking at his wife.

"I think we should give Ellie another chance to show us that she's ready to be a responsible pony owner," Mrs. Browning said.

"Yay!" Ellie threw herself at her mom and dad, but not before giving Steph the biggest grin ever. "I won't disappoint you—or Turpin!" she promised.

Steph could tell that Ellie meant every word.

"Phew! Finished at last." Steph brushed back a strand of damp hair from her forehead.

Turpin looked amazing with his new clip. Steph's fingertips still tingled faintly, but that faded as the last few violet sparkles floating around the clippers blinked out.

"Wow! He looks *fab-u-lous*! You're the best!" Ellie exclaimed. "I promise not to try anything like that ever again without mentioning it to you first!"

The two girls grinned at each other. Steph felt happy that they seemed to be becoming such good friends.

Steph gazed adoringly at Comet, who was snuffling around in the empty stall. She couldn't have done the clip without him. He was her own wonderful secret,

never to be shared with anyone else.

"And thanks for what you said to Mom and Dad. It really worked," Ellie went on. "You didn't have to go as far as promising to come here every single day."

"Just you try to keep me away!" Steph said. "Besides, my parents are going to save up to get me a new pony so, in the meantime, I've got lots of spare time."

"Well, all right. But only if you agree to ride Turpin as much as you want."

Steph's grin stretched from ear to ear. "I was hoping you'd say that!"

Ellie gave her a big hug. "There's one thing confusing me. How come you got back here so quickly earlier? I'd barely returned from the woods when you arrived."

"Oh, that. Speedy's my middle name," Steph joked. *You'd never believe me if I told you!*

Ellie linked arms with her. "Let's go into the house. Mom can make us cold drinks."

Steph was about to agree when, suddenly, she heard a sound she'd been both hoping for and dreading: the hollow thud of galloping hooves overhead.

She stiffened. Destiny! There was no mistake.

As Comet raced out of the stable, Steph pulled away from a puzzled-looking Ellie and dashed after him. "There's something I have to do. I'll follow you into the house," she said.

Just as Steph reached the paddock, a twinkling rainbow mist drifted down around her. In the center of it, Comet stood there as his true self, a black-and-white pony no longer. Bright sunlight glowed on his noble arched neck, magnificent golden wings, and cream coat. His flowing mane and tail glistened like strands of the finest gold thread.

"Comet!" Steph gasped. She had almost forgotten how beautiful he was. "Do you have to leave right now?"

Comet's deep-violet eyes softened

with affection. "I must. If I am to catch
Destiny and save her from our enemies."

Steph's throat ached with sadness as
she knew she would have to be strong. She
ran forward and threw her arms around
Comet's shining neck. Laying her cheek
against his silken warmth, she murmured
adoringly, "I'll never forget you."

"I will never forget you either, Steph,"
he whinnied softly. He allowed her to hug

him one last time, then gently moved away. "Farewell, Steph. You have been a good friend. Ride well and true," he said in a deep, musical voice.

There was a final flash of violet light and a silent explosion of rainbow glitter that sprinkled around Steph and tinkled softly as it fell to the ground. Comet spread his wings and soared upward. He faded and was gone.

Steph blinked away tears, unable to believe that everything had happened so fast. Something lay on the grass. It was a single glittering gold wing-feather. Bending down, she picked it up.

It tingled against her palm as it faded to a cream color. Steph slipped it into her pocket. She would always keep the feather to remind her of the wonderful adventure she and Comet had shared.

As she walked out of the paddock and around to the stable, Ellie appeared at the kitchen door, holding two glasses of orange juice.

A smile broke out on Steph's face as she went toward her. The rest of the summer vacation stretched ahead of her. She felt her spirits rise at the thought of countless days of shared fun with Ellie and Turpin.

"Take care, Comet. Thank you for being my friend. I hope you find Destiny and live happily together on Rainbow Mist Island," she whispered softly.

About the
AUTHOR

Sue Bentley's books for children often
include animals, fairies, and wildlife.
She lives in Northampton, England, and
enjoys reading, going to the movies, and
watching the birds on the feeders outside
her window. She loves horses, which she
thinks are all completely magical. One of
her favorite books is *Black Beauty*, which
she must have read at least ten times. At
school she was always getting scolded for
daydreaming, but she now knows that she
was storing up ideas for when she became
a writer. Sue has met and owned many
animals, but the wild creatures in her life
hold a special place in her heart.

Don't miss these Magic Ponies books!

Don't miss these Magic Puppy books!

Don't miss these Magic Kitten books!

Don't miss these Magic Bunny books!